Musician's

Monsoon

Brieanna Robertson

Whimsical Publications, LLC

Florida

Musician's Monsoon is a work of fiction. Names, characters, and incidents are the products of the author's imagination and are either fictitious or are used fictitiously. Any resemblance to actual events or persons, living or dead, is entirely coincidental.

If you purchased this book without a cover, you should be aware that this book may have been stolen property and reported as "unsold and destroyed" to the publisher. In such case, neither the publisher nor the author has received payment for this "stripped book."

To purchase the authorized electronic edition of *Musician's Monsoon*, visit www.whimsicalpublications.com

Cover art by Shyanne England
Editing by Janet Durbin

ISBN-13: 978-1-940707-88-4

Published by
Whimsical Publications, LLC
Florida

It was the last song before the encore, and Rhonda start-ed talking to the audience about how great a crowd they were. Zane seized the opportunity to take a long drink of a beer he'd had sitting on the floor. It was warm, which was gross. Not that it had been good to begin with. He decided to give it to one of the fans. He aimed for the black-haired twins because they were so into the show, but he changed his mind at the last minute when his gaze fell on that girl again.

He stepped to the edge of the stage and extended his hand, but the woman he aimed for was shoved out of the way by the blonde with the bad hair. She stretched over the barrier, extending to the point that Zane seriously thought she might dislocate her shoulders. He frowned and pulled the beer bottle just out of her grasp, then purposely held it to-ward the sandy-haired girl, who was elbowing the blonde in the ribs as she pushed her way back in again.

Zane smirked and met the woman's eyes, then indicated that he wanted to give the beer to her. She blinked, arched an eyebrow, and looked around in confusion, as if thinking he had to be motioning to someone else. He grinned and held it toward her again, giving a nod and a wink to let her know he meant her. The blonde, meanwhile, had managed to extend her arm over to him again, grasping like a seeking tentacle, and the sandy-haired woman shoved her hard, reached out, and accepted the beer bottle. She met his eyes for a second and smiled.

Zane's heart began to beat double time and he returned her smile. He chuckled under his breath when the blonde be-side her pouted like a child. He walked over to the other side of the stage and touched the hands of a few screaming fans before heading back toward the keyboard for the next song.

It was at that precise moment that he glanced back at the woman he seemed to be so enamored with, and instead of his gaze falling on her face, it fell on the blonde next to her. His eyes widened as she managed to climb over the bar-rier and, with impressive speed and strength, launched her-self onto the stage. He didn't really have time to react, and he wished he had. If his reflexes had been better, he would have run—fast.

The material masquerading as her shirt came untied and fell down. And her two behemoth breasts loomed straight at his face. All he really had time to do was put his hands up and gasp, thus inhaling a mouthful of silicone and falling backwards while she tackled him. A guitar smashed to the ground, and feedback squealed from the amp. He heard frantic footsteps all around, and he felt hands attempt to tug the Amazonian nightmare off of him, which he was grateful for...because he was suffocating.

A security guard finally managed to haul her away. Correction—*two* security guards. They yanked her off Zane, and he scrambled into a standing position before he fled to the back of the stage. His friends surrounded him, asking him if he was all right, but all he could do was shake his head and try to understand what had just happened. Death by boobs. Regardless of what any man said, that was *not* a good way to go.

"Zane!" the drummer, Billy, called. He shook him vigorously and forced Zane to look up at him. "Are you okay, man?"

Zane blinked and shook his head, trying to dispel that awful image from his mind. "Y-Yeah," he stammered. "They were so...big."

Kate and Billy exchanged a concerned glance. "Did you hit your head, dude?" Billy questioned.

He cleared his throat. "I'm fine. I was just..." He shook his head again and tried to regroup. "I'm fine. Let's finish the show."

"Are you sure?" Rhonda asked.

He nodded. "Yeah, I'm fine. I promise." He forced a smile. "That'll be something I won't forget anytime soon."

"That'll be something *none* of us will forget anytime soon," Matt grumbled.

Zane smiled, this time a little more genuinely, and he pushed away from his friends, resuming his place behind the keyboard. The crowd cheered, and he held his hands up to assure everyone he was all right. His eyes instinctively returned to the place where the sandy-haired woman was, but his heart plummeted.

She was no longer there.

Also by
Brieanna Robertson

Serendipity Series

Stand Alone Books

To the ones who rock...and who rock hard.

—Brieanna Robertson

Chapter One

"It's friggin' raining! What the heck? My hair is going to get all messed up now!"

Sophie glanced over at her cousin Lorraine and suppressed the almost overwhelming urge to roll her eyes. "Lorraine, it's Arizona in the middle of monsoon season. Of course it's raining. Just be happy it's not a dust storm."

Lorraine ignored her. "I mean, I put all this effort into looking absolutely fabulous so that I can catch Zane's attention. Now I'm going to look terrible."

Sophie clamped her mouth shut so what she wanted to say wouldn't come flying out. Lorraine already looked like a hooker. And not even one of the high-class call girls. A street-walking, right out of the ghetto in Phoenix, two-bit hooker. Her shirt could barely be classified as a shirt. More like a scrap of black material that *almost* covered her enormous, fake double Ds. Her pants were red pleather and so low that her black G-string hung out. Her platinum hair resembled something out of a bad eighties movie, and Sophie was pretty sure that if it rained too hard, Lorraine's makeup would turn her into an escaped circus clown.

Lorraine snorted and glanced down at Sophie, flipping her hair over her shoulder. "Not like you have to worry about anything," she said in her belligerent tone. "You always look the same no matter what kind of weather." She gave a high-pitched, witchy giggle. "Snow, rain, sun, it doesn't matter, you always look *bor-ing.*" She sang the last word and puffed her hair again.

Sophie heaved a sigh. Going anywhere with Lorraine was the worst form of torture. She'd rather have a root canal...she'd rather have a root canal with no Novocain. The *only* reason Sophie was here with her now was because her car had broken down immediately before the concert, and Lorraine was the only person who would go at the last minute.

None of Sophie's friends liked metal music, and they all thought *she* was ridiculous for liking it. They had some stupid notion that, because she taught orchestra and choir, she should only listen to Mozart, or Broadway hits, or something. It was dumb. So what if she taught classical music? She happened to like brash, ugly-sounding guitars and pounding drums. She spent five days a week teaching the classics. The last thing she wanted to do was listen to them on her off time too.

Lorraine snorted again. "I mean, really, what kind of attention are you going to attract in *that*?"

Sophie returned to the present and glanced down at the outfit Lorraine was mocking. She was wearing jeans and a black, fitted T-shirt with the band's logo on it. She frowned. "What are you talking about? I'm wearing the band's shirt. What's wrong with that?"

Lorraine rolled her eyes. "Wearing the band's shirt only makes you look like an obsessed fan."

Sophie raised an eyebrow. *Says the bad Pamela Anderson impersonator just reeking of "groupie,"* she thought to herself.

"If you want to catch a rock star's attention, you have to stand out." She giggled again in a girly way that made Sophie cringe.

"Well, I'm not planning on getting anyone's attention. I just want to see the show."

"Well, fine," Lorraine countered. "Better for me anyway." She laughed. "Not that you'd be any competition." She squeezed Sophie's arm like she was teasing, but Sophie knew better.

The doors to the venue opened right as they arrived, and everyone filed in mechanically. People shot Lorraine all kinds of horrified and amused glances. Sophie tried not to notice. She was actually trying very hard to pretend like she didn't even know her.

By some weird miracle, she and Lorraine managed to find a spot directly in front of the stage. Sophie was elated for half a second before Lorraine wedged her way right in front of her, thus almost blocking her view with her enormous hair. Sophie let out a frustrated growl and shuffled off to the side, situating herself in a better position. Shadows Rising was her favorite band, and she'd had to sacrifice her sanity to even make it to the concert. She refused to be thwarted by her cousin's street-walker hair.

She put her own sandy brown hair up in a ponytail and scowled at nothing in particular, recalling Lorraine's never-ending assault on her looks and character. They'd driven down from Flagstaff to see the concert in Tempe. That was roughly four hours of listening to Lorraine bash her in every way imaginable in her fake, I-mean-well tone.

Lorraine fancied herself a great beauty of supermodel proportions. In reality, the only kind of beauty competitions she'd ever win were the ones designed for drag queens. The woman wore more makeup than Sophie could comprehend. She wondered what Lorraine's face *actually* looked like. She was pretty sure her complexion wasn't really orange. And she knew the two slugs on her face that passed for lips weren't real. The woman looked like Barbie on crack.

But she thought she was gorgeous. And she got supreme enjoyment out of criticizing Sophie because she didn't lather on the cosmetics or dress like a hoochie. Sophie was just glad she was immune to Lorraine's taunting. She knew she was no great beauty. She was short and nondescript, easily lost in a crowd, with an average shade of brown hair and freckles. She didn't think she was unattractive really, but probably ranked about a five on the hot scale. Not hot, but not *not*. Sophie was the poster girl for all the people who lived in the middle of the spectrum. She didn't mind. Scoring a celebrity for a husband wasn't part of her agenda. Neither was scoring a husband at all, actually. She enjoyed her life and was content with what she had.

But Lorraine sure got a kick out of beating her down as much as possible. Sophie had a feeling that Lorraine's self-esteem was terribly low beneath her arrogant façade. It was the only reason for all the pancake makeup and her plastic surgery. How much liposuction had she had now? She'd had two nose jobs by the time she was twenty-five. And Sophie didn't even want to think about the Botox and the collagen injections.

With another sigh, Sophie folded her arms and waited for the show to start. She wasn't going to say anything to Lorraine, because all she'd end up hearing was a never-ending stream of insults, but she was secretly ecstatic that she would be able to see Zane Blake so close up. The man was a creative genius, in her opinion. While the band members helped compile the lyrics, Zane wrote all of the music himself. It was beautiful, and something about it called to Sophie's soul, almost like she could feel his emotions in the notes of his songs. She looked forward to seeing him play them live.

Was it bad to play all of your songs like you were on autopilot? Probably. Zane wondered if everyone in the audience could tell how out of it he felt. He glanced out over them while his fingers flew across the keys he loved, the keys that had brought him his dreams, his fame, everything he'd ever wanted in life.

The crowd moved like the sea, stabbing their arms into the air in time with the beat of the song, screaming and shouting like they always did. He must have looked fine.

What was he thinking? Of course he looked fine. He had done this so many times over the course of the last several years that he could do it in his sleep. His band mates could wheel him out in a coma and prop him up against something and he'd still be able to play the songs. The music he'd written had become ingrained in his DNA. Maybe that was the problem. Maybe everything had become so second nature to him that he had nothing to inspire him anymore. Maybe he really had let the life consume him to the point where it was just his occupation. If that was the case, how in the world did he get his passion back?

"The music inside of me is dead."

"Dead?" their singer, Rhonda, questioned. *"Dead as in...dead?"*

He huffed and looked up into her dark eyes. "Dead as in I can't write anything," he stated. "It's gone. All the music in my head, the lyrics, everything. I can't feel anything. I can't create anything."

"Dude, you're telling us this now?" their guitar player, Matt, threw in. "We're going on stage in five minutes! I mean, no disrespect or anything, but can't we discuss this later?"

"Zane, what is it?" Rhonda prodded, kneeling down in front of him so she could look into his eyes. "What's going on with you? You haven't been yourself lately. We've all noticed it. You've been quiet and distant."

"We're supposed to record the new album after this tour ends," Matt said. "Are you trying to tell us that you don't even have any songs?"

"No, I have no songs," Zane grumbled, shooting him an annoyed expression. "What part of 'the music inside of me is dead' did you not comprehend?"

That was the conversation he'd had with his band mates right before the show. He didn't mean to take his frustration out on his friends. He just didn't know what was wrong with him. He felt bereft and confused, not understanding why his inspiration had left him. For his entire life, he'd heard and felt music within him. Now, suddenly, he heard nothing. He felt nothing. Just emptiness. And the emptiness hurt.

How could the music that made up his entire soul suddenly vanish? It made no sense. If it was writer's block, it was the writer's block from hell.

He focused on the cluster of girls in front of the stage where he stood. There was a pair of black-haired twins rocking out harder than probably every other person in the room. He grinned, and his gaze wandered to the frightening blonde woman next to them who kept screaming his name and reaching her arms over the barrier. She hollered extra loud when she saw his eyes scan the crowd, and he suppressed a grimace.

He began to look back at his keyboard, but he did a double-take when a sandy-haired woman shoved the blonde out of the way and gave her a scowl that should've killed her. For some reason, his heart tripped over itself and made his fingers falter. He played about three notes completely wrong before he looked back down at his hand and remembered where he was in the song.

Kate, their bass player, moved over to stand next to him; she shot him a concerned, questioning look as she played. He met her gaze and shook his head, making a goofy face that caused her to smile. Obviously convinced he was all right and had only made a silly blunder, she bounded over to the other side of the stage.

Zane raised his eyes to the sandy-haired woman, and his heart, once again, cartwheeled in his chest. He had no idea why. By all rights, she really shouldn't have caught his attention. She didn't stand out like some of the others. And she wasn't head banging or flailing limbs. Once in a while, she'd put her hand up in the rock on sign, but mostly she just stood there bobbing her head to the beat.

For two songs, he kept his gaze on her, trying to figure out why his heart leapt to life at the sight of her and the hazy, muffled shroud he'd been living his life behind for the past few months lifted. In those moments, everything became pristine and crystal clear. He didn't only play his music, he *felt* it again.

It very well could have been the look on her face. While she didn't move her body in vigorous display like the rest of the crowd, her expression was one of complete appreciation and rapture. A small smile stayed on her lips throughout the show, and he got the distinct impression that while everyone else heard the music and liked the sound, she was really listening, like she felt it and could put her finger on the pulse of the message. Her subtle look of bliss meant more to him than anything else in the entire venue.

It was the last song before the encore, and Rhonda started talking to the audience about how great a crowd they were. Zane seized the opportunity to take a long drink of a beer he'd had sitting on the floor. It was warm, which was gross. Not that it had been good to begin with. He decided to give it to one of the fans. He aimed for the black-haired twins because they were so into the show, but he changed his mind at the last minute when his gaze fell on that girl again.

He stepped to the edge of the stage and extended his hand, but the woman he aimed for was shoved out of the way by the blonde with the bad hair. She stretched over the barrier, extending to the point that Zane seriously thought she might dislocate her shoulders. He frowned and pulled the beer bottle just out of her grasp, then purposely held it toward the sandy-haired girl, who was elbowing the blonde in the ribs as she pushed her way back in again.

Zane smirked and met the woman's eyes, then indicated that he wanted to give the beer to her. She blinked, arched an eyebrow, and looked around in confusion, as if thinking he had to be motioning to someone else. He grinned and held it toward her again, giving a nod and a wink to let her know he meant her. The blonde, meanwhile, had managed to extend her arm over to him again, grasping like a seeking tentacle, and the sandy-haired woman shoved her hard, reached out, and accepted the beer bottle. She met his eyes for a second and smiled.

Zane's heart began to beat double time and he returned her smile. He chuckled under his breath when the blonde beside her pouted like a child. He walked over to the other side of the stage and touched the hands of a few screaming fans before heading back toward the keyboard for the next song.

It was at that precise moment that he glanced back at the woman he seemed to be so enamored with, and instead of his gaze falling on her face, it fell on the blonde next to her. His eyes widened as she managed to climb over the barrier and, with impressive speed and strength, launched herself onto the stage. He didn't really have time to react, and he wished he had. If his reflexes had been better, he would have run—fast.

The material masquerading as her shirt came untied and fell down. And her two behemoth breasts loomed straight at his face. All he really had time to do was put his hands up and gasp, thus inhaling a mouthful of silicone and falling backwards while she tackled him. A guitar smashed to the ground, and feedback squealed from the amp. He heard frantic footsteps all around, and he felt hands attempt to tug the Amazonian nightmare off of him, which he was grateful for...because he was suffocating.

A security guard finally managed to haul her away. Correction—*two* security guards. They yanked her off Zane, and he scrambled into a standing position before he fled to the back of the stage. His friends surrounded him, asking him if he was all right, but all he could do was shake his head and try to understand what had just happened. Death by boobs. Regardless of what any man said, that was *not* a good way to go.

"Zane!" the drummer, Billy, called. He shook him vigorously and forced Zane to look up at him. "Are you okay, man?"

Zane blinked and shook his head, trying to dispel that awful image from his mind. "Y-Yeah," he stammered. "They were so...big."

Kate and Billy exchanged a concerned glance. "Did you hit your head, dude?" Billy questioned.

He cleared his throat. "I'm fine. I was just..." He shook his head again and tried to regroup. "I'm fine. Let's finish the show."

"Are you sure?" Rhonda asked.

He nodded. "Yeah, I'm fine. I promise." He forced a smile. "That'll be something I won't forget anytime soon."

"That'll be something *none* of us will forget anytime soon," Matt grumbled.

Zane smiled, this time a little more genuinely, and he pushed away from his friends, resuming his place behind the keyboard. The crowd cheered, and he held his hands up to assure everyone he was all right. His eyes instinctively returned to the place where the sandy-haired woman was, but his heart plummeted.

She was no longer there.

With a sadness inside him he couldn't accurately explain, he forced himself to finish up the set of songs, went out for the encore, then filed backstage with the rest of the band feeling weary and battle-worn. He grabbed a water bottle on his way to the dressing room and briefly wished it was whiskey.

"Whew!" Matt exclaimed, flopping down into a chair in their dressing room. "Well, that was not your typical performance." He ran his fingers through his unruly brown hair and made it look even messier than it already did.

Kate snorted as she sat down next to him and pulled a colored hairpiece out of her chestnut locks. "I'll say. Not every day your keyboardist gets attacked by flying cleavage."

Zane rolled his eyes. He suddenly felt like the room was closing in on him. "That woman was something else." He paced around the room restlessly for a few moments while the rest of his band mates shared everyday conversation and talked about highlights from the show. He half listened, not really paying attention. For whatever reason, he couldn't get his mind off that woman in the crowd.

"Hey, Zane. You in there, man?"

He moved away from Matt, who was waving his hand in his face. "What?"

He arched an eyebrow. "What? We're heading out. You

plan on chilling in the dressing room all night?"

Zane frowned and glanced at the rest of the band, all in the entrance of the dressing room ready to make their way to the bus. He felt antsy and his mind was muddled. He didn't want to go back to the hotel room and watch people get wasted...again. Everything inside of him felt tumultuous and chaotic. If he didn't get a moment to himself, he was going to explode.

"You guys go. I'm going to take a walk."

"By yourself?" Rhonda screeched. "At least take a security guard with you or something."

He pushed past them with a barely contained growl, needing to be out of the confined space before he lost his mind. "I'm a big boy. I think I can handle it. I'll meet you guys later."

"But Zane—"

He turned and looked back at Rhonda, forcing patience into his reply. He knew she just cared about him. "You guys, I really need to decompress. Alone. Okay? It'll be fine. I'm a celebrity—all right, great, but I'm still a person. And I'm a person who needs a second to myself to figure out what's going on inside my head. I think I'm entitled to that."

"Just let him do what he wants," Kate snapped. "I don't have time to stand around here all night babying Zane. I have things I need to take care of." She crossed her arms and scowled.

Billy and Matt exchanged a confused look at her out-of-character witchiness. "Dude, what crawled up your butt and died?" Matt grumbled.

Kate flipped him off.

Rhonda sighed visibly and focused her attention back on Zane. "All right. We're just worried about you. You haven't been—"

"Myself. I know. That's why I need to be alone. I need to figure out where my self decided to go." He pivoted on his heel and continued down the hall toward the exit. If he didn't get some kind of control over the tumult inside him, he could end up blowing his entire career.

Because, right now, none of it really seemed worth it anymore. Not when his music was gone.

Chapter Two

"Are you out of your mind?" Sophie screamed after the security guard finished dragging Lorraine out of the venue. "Are you trying to get arrested?"

Lorraine snorted as she repositioned her shirt. "Oh please," she said with a roll of her eyes. "It's not like I meant for my shirt to come off. That was a complete accident." She sniffed and tried to smooth her hair. "Besides, it's not like he minded. I mean, the guy's mouth totally latched straight on."

Sophie arched an eyebrow and folded her arms. "Given the circumstances, Lorraine, I don't think he had a choice. You were practically smothering him." She turned away from her cousin in exasperation. "That was so humiliating. I can't believe I'm even related to you."

"You can't believe you're related to *me*?" She huffed. "Whatever. At least I'm interesting."

Sophie let out a short, sarcastic laugh. "Interesting? Oh yeah, Lorraine, you're one of a kind all right." She started to walk away through the parking lot of the venue and toward the manmade lake next to it.

"Hey! Where are you going?" Lorraine shouted after her.

"Away from you!" Sophie spat back. "There are bars all along this street. Go get smashed or something. I'll find you later when I'm not totally pissed at you." She kept walking, trying to return to some kind of calm state. It was difficult to manage, considering Lorraine had completely ruined what had, quite possibly, been the best concert she'd ever attended. She didn't even get to see the end, and on the way out, she'd accidentally dropped the beer bottle Zane had given her. It had shattered all over the ground. Now she didn't even have a souvenir. And he had purposely given it to *her*. She had no idea why.

It didn't matter now anyway. It was gone, and so was

he...and what a beautiful man. He was breathtaking on stage with his long, golden hair and his commanding presence. She wondered what he'd be like in person. He always seemed so approachable in the interviews she'd seen of him.

She shook her head. Well, she'd never know, so what good was it to ponder on it? She stuffed her hands in her pockets and wandered aimlessly as the hot Arizona day turned into a sultry Arizona night. The monsoon had passed, traveling east, leaving a humid, sweltering, almost sensual night in its wake.

She sighed and meandered for a while, replaying what she had seen of the show in her mind and trying to relive it.

After a good forty-five minutes, she had calmed sufficiently, but her anger had been replaced with a dull kind of sorrow and a strange loneliness that was foreign to her. She never felt lonely. She was independent, self-sufficient, and enjoyed her life. She had no idea where the sudden wave of sadness came from, but out of nowhere, the thing she wanted more than anything in the world was to have someone look at her the way Zane Blake had from the stage. Like she was actually something special and not just a face in the crowd. Who cared if he was only a great performer and interacted well with his fans? He'd made her feel special. Period. And she hadn't realized until now how insignificant she usually felt.

Regardless of the fact that he would never remember her past the moment he had handed her his beer, Zane had made her feel like a glittering jewel sitting in the middle of a bunch of sand.

With a sigh, she turned and strode back to the venue, which was now all but deserted. She headed toward Lorraine's car, but stopped and frowned. She wasn't ready to go find her delinquent cousin. Her aggravation was still too strong. Maybe she would walk down the street and see what she could see. It was the main downtown strip in Tempe, right next to the university. Plus, it was a Friday night. If nothing else, she could at least find something to eat. She was beyond famished.

Casting one more glance back at Lorraine's car, her gaze fell on the stupid antenna ball. It was the girliest thing she'd ever seen. A smiley face with a blonde ponytail, gigantic sunglasses and a pink headband that said *Princess* on it in gold sparkly writing. It even had lips the size of Lorraine's, painted an obnoxious shade of red. At that moment, Sophie hated the antenna ball with a fury that rivaled the Arizona monsoon. It looked like Lorraine, and she was the one who had ruined a concert Sophie had been waiting to see for a small eternity. Since she couldn't physically do anything to her cousin, she took her rage out on the ball.

She yanked it off the antenna and thumped it against the side of the car a few times before turning and pitching it MLB-player style. She didn't look to see if anyone was around, and she almost had an all-out heart attack as her fingers released the ball and her gaze traveled past it to see Zane Blake, of all people, standing directly in its intended path. Her eyes bulged, and she drew in a deep breath to shout out a warning, but it all happened too quickly.

The antenna ball connected—with great force—against his right eye.

The warning Sophie would have shouted turned into a scream of horror, and her hands flew up to cover her mouth as he staggered backwards and let out a slew of curse words. He held his hand to his eye and bent over.

"Oh my gosh!" Sophie cried. "I am *so sorry*!" She glanced around and started over to him, wondering where he had even come from. There was no one anywhere. It was just her luck.

He heaved a sigh and braced one hand on his knee. "What was that? A friggin' baseball?" he muttered. "I'm gonna have to rock a pirate patch now. Son of a..." He looked up at her as she approached, but kept his hand over his eye. The eye that wasn't injured was remarkably green, and it widened considerably. "You!"

Sophie winced. "Yeah, it was me. I am so sorry." She picked the ball up, holding it up for him to see. "Not a baseball. Antenna ball." She felt like the world's biggest imbecile.

He frowned and stood straight, still keeping his hand over his eye. "Dang, what did that antenna ball ever do to you? More importantly, what did *I* ever do to you?"

A warm flush crept into her cheeks, and she shook her head. "I was angry. Where did you come from? I didn't even see you!"

He snorted. "Yeah, kind of hard to see past the red haze of rage."

Her face grew even warmer, and she averted her gaze. "I am so sorry," she repeated, for lack of anything better. "Let me see. I didn't do any permanent damage, did I?" She stood on her tiptoes while he tried to force his watering eye open, and she inspected it to the best of her ability. "It looks okay, just red," she surmised.

"Imagine that," he muttered.

She looked back up at him, and for one stupid second, her heartbeat faltered. The shock of the situation began to abate as reality seeped in. It wasn't every day a person got to stand in front of and talk to one of their all-time favorite rock stars. "I really am sorry," she said again, her voice growing softer and meeker than she would have liked. She instinctively retreated, feeling like she was standing too close to him.

He shook his head, sending a ripple through his golden mane of hair. A small, mischievous smile played about his full lips, and she was suddenly struck dumb by the sheer, masculine beauty of him. He looked like a Viking, tall and powerful with features strong enough to be undeniably manly, but not harsh enough to look fierce. She felt smaller and more insignificant than she ever had in her life standing beside his dominant presence.

His gaze locked with hers, and his small smile grew bigger. He folded his arms over his chest and cocked his head to one side in a flirty, playful manner. "Well, I think you're going to have to make that up to me," he stated. "Unless you were intentionally trying to make me the one-eyed keyboardist."

Her face flamed with humiliation, and she rolled her eyes. "Good lord, and after Lorraine attacked you on stage? I'm like Murphy's Law tonight."

Both of his eyebrows shot up. "You knew that crazy woman?"

Sophie winced again and scrunched her nose up. "She's kind of my cousin." She held her hands up. "Related by blood, not by choice." She shook her head. "I can't believe she did that."

"It was horrifying."

He stated it so flat and bland that Sophie burst into giggles, which only succeeded in making her feel more idiotic than she already did. She covered her face with her hands until she got herself under control. Once successful, she looked up at him again. His gorgeous grin disarmed her.

"See, now you *have* to make it up to me," he said. "You catch my attention in a sea of people and distract me to where I can't even play my own song. *Then* your psycho cousin tries to assassinate me with her chest."

A laugh tore from Sophie's throat before she could stop it.

Zane took a step closer to her. "*Then* you disappear from the crowd and apparently discard the beer I gave you." He made a disgusted noise and rolled his eyes. "Some kind of fan you are."

Her mouth fell open in feigned offense. "I didn't discard it! Someone crashed into me and I dropped it! I couldn't exactly pick up the pieces and put them on my wall like a warped mosaic."

He waved his hand as if her words were meaningless. He took another step closer until their bodies almost touched. "*Then* you try and put out my eye. That's a long list."

She smirked at him, and some of her self-consciousness dissipated at his teasing. Heat radiated from his body, and it made electric tingles run along her skin. He was sexy, smooth, and playful...and a musical genius. She would be lying to herself if she tried to deny her attraction to him. Heck, she had always been attracted to him in posters and TV interviews. Standing this close to him in person was just that much more powerful.

She put her hand on her hip and tried to seem cocky. "Yeah, well what do you want, music man?" It came out more of a sarcastic challenge than she had meant.

He arched an eyebrow in surprise. His green eyes stared into hers for several heartbeats of silence. She expected a quick, snappy response to leave his lips, something tinged in arrogance that would prove the fact that women never turned him down. It was what she expected, but not what she received.

Instead, his eyes turned soft, scanning her face in a glance that was brief, but left warmth in its wake. "My muse," he murmured.

She frowned. "Excuse me?"

"What I want is my muse." He reached out and placed his hands gently on her shoulders. The air caught in her throat, making it impossible for her to draw in a decent breath. He bent his head and brought his mouth to her ear. "Inspire me," he whispered.

Her heart began to beat out erratic patterns, and delicious, sensuous tremors ran along her spine. The breathy laugh that left her sounded foreign to her ears and would have embarrassed her if she hadn't been concentrating so hard on the waves of warmth passing between the two of them. "I make no promises," she managed to get out.

He pulled back and grinned down at her. "You don't understand. There's a reason I singled you out in the crowd. I don't know why, but when I look at you, I hear music."

She blinked. Dang. If that was a line, it sure was a good one. Worked for her. She bit her bottom lip, at a loss for words, and suppressed a shiver as one of his hands descended along her bare arm and played idly with her fingers.

"I'd like to explain," he continued.

She met his gaze and nodded like a mute. Really, what was she supposed to do? Tell him no? Yeah, right.

If it was possible, his stunning grin grew even brighter. His fingers tightened on hers. "Do you have a name?" he prodded.

She cleared her throat and tried to remember how to function like a normal human. "Um, Sophie," she replied.

"Sophie," he repeated. "I'm Zane."

She snorted. "No crap." She couldn't swear. She was too used to teaching kids. Euphemisms were her best friends, even if they sounded slightly lame in situations, say, like this one.

He chuckled and tugged on her hand, pulling her closer to him. "Have dinner with me."

It wasn't a request, wasn't a question, and she knew she would hate herself if she said no. Part of her was skeptical; part of her didn't understand. She was plain. She was ordinary. Why was he flirting with her when he could have been at some after-party kegger with a bunch of hot blondes?

"Because hot blondes are average at best," he stated.

She blinked in bewilderment, looked up at him, and felt the color leave her face when she realized she'd spoken her thoughts aloud.

"And you're not plain," he continued. "Not in the least. If

you were plain, I never would have noticed you. You stood out in the crowd, Sophie. Your face made me falter in my playing. Your *lovely* face. A plain person wouldn't cause that reaction."

Her mouth and throat went dry, thus preventing her from speaking. So, instead, she just stared at him like a moron. She counted her heartbeats as they thundered in her chest. *One...two...three...four....*

Four beats and her senses returned. She shook her head and backed away from him. "Dude," she stated, sounding entirely too much like one of her high school students. "What the heck is this?" She looked around the still-deserted parking lot and wondered what kind of alternate universe she had fallen into.

She pulled her fingers out of his grasp and slashed the air with her hands. The delightful electrical current that had been passing between them dissipated as she moved away.

"This is insane." She fixed him with a critical eye and put one hand on her hip while she brandished the antenna ball with the other. "Reality check," she said. "This kind of stuff never happens to people like me. What are you up to?" He raised his eyebrows and opened his mouth to speak, but she cut him off by taking a daring step up to him and stabbing the now frazzled-looking antenna ball at him. "You said you wanted to explain all that mumbo jumbo about hearing music when you looked at me. So get to it, because I swear, if you're just trying to put a notch on your belt for laughs, or someone made a bet with you or something like that, so help me, I will put out your other eye."

He held his hands up and retreated slightly. "Whoa, calm down!" he exclaimed. "No one bet me anything!"

"Then what are you telling me all this junk for?" She shook the ball at him again. "I'm a nobody, a forgettable face in the crowd. You say hot blondes are average at best? What, are you on crack? Do you honestly expect me to believe that you actually feel that way, or do you think I'm a gullible idiot? Well, let me tell you something, mister. I've been around long enough to know that men like you, who do what you do, do *not* try to pick up girls like me without some kind of motive. So what's yours?" She flung the ball down again. It bounced once on the asphalt and rolled away in dejection. As if to punctuate her sentence, thunder rumbled ominously in the distance. Sophie put her hands on her hips and stared up at him in a blatant challenge.

Zane seemed completely at a loss, and he took a breath to say something, but whatever it was disappeared while a look of surprised awe passed over his face. His eyes widened, and he gasped softly before his attention snapped to her. He reached down to snatch her wrist. "Come with me," he stated.

Sophie's eyes bulged when he turned and started to haul her after him across the parking lot. Suddenly, every bad horror movie she had ever seen flashed through her mind and she screamed. "What? Where?"

"My hotel," he threw over his shoulder. "I hear all sorts of notes. I need to get them down!"

"Your *hotel*?" she gasped. "No way! Abduction!" She dug in her heels, trying to pull out of his grasp, her mind turning wildly with terrible scenarios. She couldn't help it. Before she'd taught high school, she'd taught elementary, where she had been inundated with what to do if one was being kidnapped. "Stranger danger!" she shouted. "Let me go!" She tried to re-member self-defense, but everything in her mind was mud-dled and confused. Some of the anger she'd felt toward the antenna ball resurfaced at the fact that he was blatantly ignor-ing her demands. "I said, *let go*!" She used the side of her hand to karate chop him on the neck like she'd seen in the movies. Maybe it would incapacitate him, or knock him out, or—

"Ow!" he cried. "What the—" He let go of her wrist. He put his hand to his neck and turned slowly toward her. His glower was icy, but also mixed with bafflement.

She swallowed hard. Or, maybe the whole karate-chop thing would just piss him off. Something in her head told her to run, so she turned to do just that, but he was faster. He grasped her around the wrist again, and she shrieked as he yanked her up close to his body. She crashed into his un-yielding chest and all the air left her, not from force, but from the shock of the smoldering desire that flared to life within her body.

"Gimme a break!" he exclaimed. He still had a tight hold on her arm.

She stole a tentative glance up into his eyes of green fire.

He let out an annoyed sigh and shook his head. "You just kung-fooed me in the neck!"

She wrinkled her brow, unsure of what to say or how to react.

"I am not *abducting* you," he persisted. "I wanted to take you back to my hotel because that's where my instruments are. My band already left right after the show. They took off in the bus. I told them, as well as all of my security, to leave me the hell alone because I wanted to be by myself for once. I wanted to walk so I could try and get a certain woman out of my head who distracted me to a fault during the show."

Sophie's cheeks burned once again.

"By random chance, that same woman tried to blind me in the parking lot and, for some reason, her fiery temper and amazing blue eyes make me hear chords." His voice softened, and he sighed, taking her chin in his free hand. "I'm not taking you to an abandoned warehouse to murder you. I got excited for a second because I haven't been able to hear any music for months now. Forgive me for having a creative moment." His fingers left her chin and spanned across the column of her throat.

Sophie closed her eyes as the warmth of his palm settled over the pulse in her neck. She had to fight not to tremble.

"Your heart is racing," he continued, his voice sultry and sinful even in its sincerity. "I'm sorry I startled you. You just...you don't understand." He closed his eyes and let out a long, slow breath. He fixed his gaze on her again and smiled softly. "You're absolutely right. I need to explain myself." Zane traced the outline of her mouth and along her jawline, as if studying the texture of her skin. "I have been all over the world. I've met tons of fans and numerous gorgeous women. None of them radiated the same gentle, warm light that I saw coming from you during the show. It caught my attention from the stage because it seemed so genuine. You weren't doing everything in your power to get noticed like your freaky cousin. You were just standing there, enjoying my music, the music that comes straight from the depths of my soul. It made me feel different. Not like a rock star."

She frowned thoughtfully. "But you *are* a rock star."

He shook his head. "No, I'm a *musician*. There's a difference, but I think the two blended into one for a while, and I forgot where the musician ended and the celebrity began. It numbed me, made me apathetic, and I couldn't create anymore. It's been horrible..."

"I love your music," she blurted. "It's...I don't know how to explain it. I don't only hear it. I feel it, too... It feels like magic. Like euphoria." She felt stupid for her words, but she thought maybe he needed to hear them. He'd just revealed something incredibly personal. The least she could do was give him some reassurance. "I love your music above all others. It sounds the way I feel inside."

His grin rivaled the Arizona lightning. "That is the best thing you could have said to me."

He closed his eyes with a blissful expression and began to hum a soft melody. It was barely discernable, and she leaned closer out of sheer curiosity. "What is that?" she asked softly.

His chuckle reminded her of the rolling thunder in the distance, and it heated her blood. "It's you," he whispered. At her quizzical frown, he smiled. "I meant what I said, about hearing music. Your irritation was like a crashing cymbal. When you smiled, I imagined a slow, seductive bass line."

She blushed again, much to her dismay, and frowned because she didn't know what else to do. "Why in the world would my smile inspire *that?*"

He took the opportunity to slip an arm around her waist. "Because you're sexy!" His grin reflected both teasing and sincerity.

Her face grew even hotter, and she let her breath out in a huff. She was probably going to remain in a permanent state of red after this. "Right, whatever."

"I mean it!" he continued. "You have lovely eyes, and these are adorable." He played a quick game of connect the dots with the freckles across her nose. "I especially enjoy these." He grazed his fingers over the dimples in her cheeks. "And you're just small enough to fit perfectly in my arms." He shrugged one shoulder in a lazy, confident gesture. "Besides..." He reached behind her head to tug the tie out of her hair. It spilled free around her shoulders, and he ran his fingers through it. She marveled over the rapturous expression on his face. "Even your hair is made of notes." He let the strands fall through his fingers and whispered chords as they cascaded down. "A...E...G..." He shook his head. "Incredible."

She felt awkward under his scrutiny and didn't know how to handle the kind of things he said to her, so she desperately tried to make a stab at humor. "Well, I guess if anyone would be made of music, it would have to be me. I *do* teach choir and orchestra."

Instead of rolling his eyes at her pathetic excuse for witticism, he gave her a warm, beautiful grin while he continued to thread his slender fingers through her hair. "Well, that does make sense, doesn't it?"

This was insane. She had no idea if he was serious, or if he was handing her a line. Sophie was a practical person, a rational person. She wasn't necessarily the most spontaneous, so random occurrences in which famous rock stars tried to tell her she inspired music and then attempted to haul her back to a hotel were slightly out of her element. She knew she wasn't beautiful, not worthy of inspiring much of anything except maybe obedience from her students when she lost her temper, so either this dude was out of his mind, or he was full of it.

Odds were, he was full of it. But it was weird that he would be trying to pick *her* up, of all people. If he just wanted to get lucky, he could go down the street and have his pick of any number of hot women at one of the bars along Mill Avenue. Why bother with her at all? There was the fact that she had tried to detach his retina with an antenna ball, but that should have annoyed him, not intrigued him. None of this made any kind of sense whatsoever. It defied every social rule she knew about.

Which led her to believe that maybe he wasn't full of it after all.

That meant he had to be out of his mind. Only logical explanation.

He raised an eyebrow as he studied her expression. "What in the world is going on inside your head?" he questioned.

She glanced up at him. "Why, you smell smoke and burning rubber?"

Amusement flashed over his features. "You're a teacher, so I hope not. I would assume you're usually pretty good about using your gray matter."

She shrugged. "Depends on the day."

A gentle smile curved his lips, and he removed his fingers

from her hair to trail them lightly down her bare arms as he took a step away from her. "I'm coming on too strong. I apologize. People always tell me I'm too aggressive and too impulsive."

The moist heat of the night suddenly felt cold as it filled the distance he had put between them, and she found some crazy part of her longing for his all-consuming presence again. She shook her head and tried to make her mind stop spinning long enough to form a coherent thought. "I wouldn't necessarily call you aggressive. Impulsive, maybe." She smirked up at him. "You're not used to people, women especially, telling you no either."

His brow furrowed and he averted his gaze, looking genuinely troubled by her words. "That's not what this is about, Sophie. I haven't said all of this to you because I'm trying to hook up with you, and the fact that you didn't melt at my feet isn't some kind of challenge. Maybe I'm a rock star, but I'm still a man, a unique individual. Please don't define my personality based on my occupation."

His rebuke wasn't harsh, but it was powerful regardless. Self-loathing washed over her at the fact that she had summed him up and judged him when she knew nothing about him. "I'm sorry, Zane. I didn't mean to do that. I just..." She swallowed the lump of shame that had lodged in her throat. "Things like this don't happen to me."

He met her gaze and smirked. "You said that already."

She held her arms out at her sides helplessly. "Well, it's true! I'm a nobody! I'm practically invisible most of the time. The things you're saying to me are like a foreign language."

"Stop saying negative things about yourself," he said as he reached out to take her hand. "It's bothering me." He pulled her back into the circle of his arm, and Sophie's breath vanished as her senses once again filled with his warmth, the solidness of his body, and the smell of lingering cologne mixed with beer and sweat. That should have been gross to her, but it wasn't.

"I had no way of knowing you would deny my advances when I glimpsed you from the stage. At that point, I wasn't planning on making any advances. It's very simple, Sophie. My passion vanished. I don't know why. You brought it back. I don't know why that is either. I just know it's true."

He brought his lips to hover right above hers, enough so his breath tickled her mouth. Her heart did all kinds of acrobatics, and any trepidation she'd had before was obliterated by a complete and unadulterated craving for the man in front of her. He had always epitomized passion to her, the way he composed, the way he played. To have him standing so close, touching her the way he was, made her feel like she had fallen into some kind of strange fantasy. She closed her eyes and, without even meaning to, her free hand crept up to rest against his shoulder.

No one had ever looked at her the way Zane had from the stage, the way he continued to look at her now. Not plain, uninteresting, average Sophie. He made her feel like a goddess. Her common sense told her that was ridiculous and that he was probably still just trying to get into her pants, but the expression on his face said otherwise. So did her heart. And she'd always been an exceptional judge of character.

"Sophie," he purred.

"Hmmm?"

"I'd like to try something, but I'm afraid you'll hit me." He rested his forehead against hers and grinned. "And I get the distinct feeling you're one of those girls who doesn't kiss on the first date."

A shiver trickled down her spine at the thought of kissing Zane. She instinctively pressed closer to him, wanting more of the delicious heat his strong body emitted. "Who says this is a date?" she whispered.

He pulled away enough to look down at her. "Oh, that's right. It was an assault that turned into an abduction."

She laughed, and the jubilation put her at ease. Her palm rested on his shoulder, close to the base of his neck, and she felt his pulse. It hammered almost as hard as hers. She shook her head in wonderment. "You're really not full of crap, are you?" she murmured.

He gave her an easy, irresistible smile. "No, I'm not."

She sighed and decided not to think about any of this, or second-guess it, or be *boring,* as Lorraine would call her. She reached her fingers over to the spot on his neck she had tried to hatchet and rubbed the muscle there in soothing circles. He tilted his head to grant her access and closed his eyes in contentment. She smiled. "I'm sorry I attacked you...twice...after Lorraine tried to pile-drive you on stage."

Zane took her hand in his and placed a lingering kiss on her palm. "Make it up to me." His smile reflected all devilish mirth.

Far off along the horizon, lightning illuminated the darkness, and thunder rolled ominously from one side of the desert sky to the other. It caught their attention, and Zane grinned. "Nature's rock concert," he murmured.

Sophie watched him for several quiet moments, taking in his beauty, both physically and in what he was showing her of his soul. She let out a tremulous breath and whispered his name. Really, what did she have to lose? Her life had been greatly devoid of sinful fantasies. She deserved at least one, didn't she?

When he looked back at her, she raised herself on her toes and wrapped her arms around his neck, pressing her body to his as their lips met. He sucked his breath in and made a happy noise in his throat before he took her face in his hands and returned the kiss eagerly. His lips were softer than anything she had ever felt, and they played over hers with expertise she lacked. It was intimidating, yet extremely sexy. He gently deepened the kiss, and as his tongue slid along hers, a groan escaped Sophie and everything inside her ignited.

She slid her palms down his chest and gripped the fabric of his shirt in her fists as his lips and tongue teased and played with hers. Heat coiled within her, and infernal desire like she had never known swept through her like a violent storm. She had always been a reserved person, a relatively cautious person. She didn't recognize herself right now, or her reactions to him. She didn't care. When was the last time she'd had any kind of an adventure? Oh, right. Never.

He pulled away with a long, slow exhale, but his arms slid around her and he tucked her close against his chest as he rested his cheek on top of her head. "That's exactly what I thought it would be," he breathed.

She tugged on her bottom lip with her teeth and tried to calm her pounding heart. She closed her eyes and relished the warm protection she felt cocooned in his embrace. "Which is?"

"A musical masterpiece."

"Sophie? Sophie, where did you go?"

Sophie bristled as Lorraine's whiny, slightly slurred speech sliced across the otherwise peaceful parking lot. "Great," Sophie grumbled. "Hurry, before she tries to kill you again." She grabbed Zane's hand and tugged him around to hide behind the far wall of the venue.

Zane chuckled and remained near Sophie, keeping one arm wrapped loosely around her waist. "I feel like a teenager hiding from a parent," he said.

Sophie snorted. "Even that would be a more pleasant situation. Seriously, if she sees me with you, she's gonna flip, and I don't want to hear it. That, and she'll probably attach herself to your leg or something."

He laughed and tightened his arm, bringing her close. "What do you suggest?" He whispered against her ear and nuzzled his lips at the base of her neck.

Sophie's knees almost buckled, but to her credit, she remained upright. She glanced back at Lorraine, who wandered aimlessly, then turned to Zane, feeling mischievous and free. "You up for an adventure?"

He arched an eyebrow. "Always."

"Do you have a little bit of time before you have to hit the road again?"

"We're here for a day."

She grinned and placed her palms against his chest. "She's drunk, so she won't move that fast. I can steal her car. She'll find her way to a hotel."

He stared at her in shock. Gradually, his surprise melted into amusement. "Bad teacher," he teased.

She shrugged. "I have my moments." Actually, she usually didn't, but now seemed like a good time to start. She bit her lip. "You game?"

His gaze softened, and he cupped her cheek in his palm, feathering his thumb across her lip. "Where are we going?"

"Let's go chase the storm," she said in excitement. "Get a front row seat to nature's rock concert."

The way he looked at her melted her heart in a dangerous way, and she knew she was in trouble when it came to this man. But, for some reason, it was okay. It felt right, somehow.

He reached for her hand and squeezed, giving her a smile that said a thousand things. "Ready when you are."

Chapter Three

Sophie screamed as she and Zane made a mad dash toward Lorraine's car. The parking lot was pretty well abandoned, so they had a straight shot, but Lorraine caught on faster than Sophie had been anticipating.

"Sophie?" Lorraine called right as the two of them reached the car. She wobbled in their direction. "What are you doing? Who are you—Oh my gosh!" With superhuman speed and more agility than she should have possessed at that moment, Lorraine started sprinting across the parking lot. "What are you doing with Zane Blake?" she screeched. "Was he looking for me? Zane! Here I am!"

Sophie fumbled with the keys while Zane tugged on the door handle of the passenger car, not that that would do any good.

"Hurry up!" he half shouted, half laughed. "Someone let the freak out of the circus, and she's coming straight for me!"

Sophie laughed so hard she snorted, and she dropped the keys in the process.

"Sophie!" Zane cried. "You've already tried to kill me twice tonight. Whatever I did to piss you off so badly, I'm sorry! Just don't hand me over to your cousin. I'm begging you!" He yanked on the door handle again while Lorraine let out a hair-raising banshee shriek.

Sophie messed around with the keys while laughing and finally managed to yank the door open. She jumped in and reached over to unlock the passenger door right as Lorraine got to the car. Zane all but vaulted in and slammed the door, locking it for good measure.

Sophie turned the key in the ignition, and Lorraine ran around to her side to pound on the window. "Sophie! What are you doing? Stealing my car? Why are you with Zane

Blake? Are you for real right now? Or am I really just *that* drunk?" She staggered away from the car with a hyena-like cackle. "I have to be hallucinating, because I know my stupid, boring, plain Jane cousin would be the last person to attract the attention of a *rock star*!" She laughed again. "This is a joke, right? Am I on camera somewhere? Am I being *Punk'd*?" She stumbled around the parking lot shouting for the nonexistent camera crew to come out.

Sophie's hands froze on the steering wheel and, for one humiliating moment, she fought tears. She didn't know why, but right then, the words Lorraine had always hurled at her hurt worse than they ever had. Maybe because Zane had almost had her believing she was something special for half a second.

What was she even doing here with him? This was stupid. She should go back home. Take him to his hotel and then drive back to Flagstaff with her heinous cousin. Go on with her life—her *boring* life—and just teach school and go about her routine. That was safe. That was normalcy. She wasn't the type of person for whirlwind adventure. Not rational, teacher Sophie.

Zane made a strange growling noise in his throat that brought Sophie out of her thoughts long enough to frown and question his actions as he pushed the passenger door open and got out of the car. "Where are you going?" she called. He ignored her, but she saw him pull out his cell phone and stab in a number, mumble something, then stab in another number.

He strode around the car and she heard him mutter, "I need a cab at the Marquee Theatre, please. Now."

Her heart fell even more. He was done with her. He'd probably finally realized that what Lorraine said was true. He shouldn't be wasting his time with her.

She jumped when her door opened and he held his hand out to her. She looked up at him in confusion.

He smiled softly, stuffed his phone back in his pocket, and waited.

Slowly, more out of morbid curiosity than anything else, she slid her hand into his. He eased her back out of the car and said nothing, but placed the sweetest kiss to her cheek before turning and heading back toward her cousin.

"Hey!" he called.

Lorraine spun so fast she almost fell over. "Zane!" she shouted. She ambled over to him, giggling ridiculously, and Zane reached out to grasp her shoulders and stop her from crashing into him. "Hey, sexy." She went for a purr, but it came out a slur. "That's a record for Sophie. Usually, guys get bored with her after only three minutes instead of five."

Sophie saw tension coil through Zane's broad shoulders, and he snatched Lorraine's wrist before she could roam her questing hand across his chest. "Look," he spat out. "I'm only going to say this to you once, so it would be in your best interests if you paid attention." He turned and started to stride back toward the theater, dragging Lorraine along behind him. "I have no desire to be in the company of a trashy drunk woman with more plastic parts than flesh and blood ones. However, I also don't feel right letting my date's cousin wander the street a hot mess, so here's the way it's going to go down. I called you a cab. You're going to get in it. I'm putting you in a nice room at the Marriott. Sleep it off and get over yourself."

With impeccable timing, the taxi showed up right as Zane reached the front entrance. Sophie followed behind at a safe distance.

"Wait, what?" Lorraine grumbled. Then her blurry eyes lit up. "Oh, we're going straight to the hotel then? You move fast."

She tried to grope him again, but he restrained her. "*We* are not going anywhere. *You* are going to the hotel by yourself. Sophie and I are going to go enjoy our date." He opened up the back door of the cab.

"You and *Sophie*?" she hollered. "This really is some kind of joke, isn't it?"

He sneered at her, his disgust more than apparent. "The only joke I see around here is you." He all but pushed her into the cab and slammed the door, then told the driver where to take her and handed him some money.

Sophie stared, shocked, as the cab drove off with her inebriated and obnoxious cousin. She slid her gaze over to Zane, who had his back to her. He stood tall, strong, his blond hair cascading down to his mid-back. Stick him in some medieval attire, put a sword in his hand, and he really would have looked like a warrior of old. She swallowed hard, and her heart skipped a beat as he looked at her over his shoulder.

She saw his shoulders move in a sigh before he walked back over to stand in front of her.

"I apologize for all of that," he murmured.

She blinked in bewilderment. "Why did you do that?" Her voice came out in a breathy wisp of sound.

His brilliant green eyes met hers. "I told you it bothered me when you said negative things about yourself. It apparently bothers me worse when other people say negative things about you."

"B-But why? You don't even know me." Her mind was spinning wildly out of control, and she was having difficulty processing anything that was currently happening.

"Does it matter?"

"I just...I'm pretty used to defending myself most of the time."

He shrugged. "Everyone needs a champion once in a while."

She stared at him for a long moment, long enough that he arched an eyebrow and started to look self-conscious. Then, she did something so out of character she wondered what kind of weird magic was in the air tonight. She slid her palms up his chest and linked her fingers behind his neck, all but attacking his lips with hers in a fervent kiss.

He responded instantly, slipping his arms around her to pull her tight and close against him. He dominated her mouth until she was dizzy and gasping. When she pulled away, she buried her face against his shoulder and closed her eyes, relishing his warmth and his strength, wanting to soak it into herself so she'd always remember.

His chuckle vibrated through her as he stroked his hands down her hair. "Now, you see, Sophie, *that* was anything but boring."

She felt her face flame, so she snuggled closer to him in order to hide her complete embarrassment at her forwardness. He didn't seem to mind. "This kind of stuff never happens to me," she mumbled into his shirt.

"That's the third time you've said that tonight."

She finally pulled away to look up at him. "Well, it keeps getting weirder!"

A mischievous smile played around his lips. "Well, I'm not the one who put out my eye, karate chopped me in the neck, and then attacked my mouth right now. That's all you. I'm just trying to go with the flow. Your cousin has to be smoking something because this is, by far, the least boring night I've ever had."

Sophie's heart did something funny at his words, something dangerous. The last thing she needed to do was become attached to a famous musician. That had disaster written all over it. But regardless of what her common sense told her, if Zane kept saying such nice things to her, she was going to be in trouble.

She didn't have much time to contemplate this because he nuzzled his lips against the side of her neck and her ear and she lost all rational thought. "You smell like cherry blossoms," he murmured. "It's driving me insane."

Her face burned for, what, the ten-millionth time that night? She pulled back slightly and looked up at him. "Courtesy of Bath and Body Works."

He raised his eyebrows and grinned. "Just an FYI, a *boring* woman wouldn't wear such sexy fragrances."

She rolled her eyes. "Okay, would you stop it with that? I'm going to blush myself into the ground."

He laughed softly and slipped an arm around her waist so she couldn't get away. "I'm just trying to tell you..." He pushed back some rogue strands of her sandy hair and gazed down into her eyes, all traces of teasing vanishing. He sighed. "Sophie, I don't know what you've been led to believe you're whole life, or who's told you that you were boring, but it's BS. All of it." He traced the line of her jaw and the column of her throat with his fingers. "If you're not too tired of me yet, I think there may still be some storm for us to chase. You still up for it?"

"Of course I am." She didn't recognize the sensual, breathy tone of her own voice, and she definitely didn't recognize this new impulsive part of her that had been dormant for the first thirty years of her life. But, for some reason, she didn't hate it. In all reality, it was kind of exhilarating.

Zane's grin should have illuminated the entire parking lot. He reached down and took her hand. "All right, let's go. I'm hungry. Are you?" At her nod, he squeezed her fingers and led her back to Lorraine's car. "I'm pretty sure the only thing open right now is Jack in the Box, and if we're going to catch up to the storm, we'd better get it to go. Is that okay? I know it's not romantic, but..."

Sophie giggled. "Zane, I'm a teacher, and I'm single. Do you know how many nights a week I eat takeout? It's not a big deal, I promise."

He laughed, stopped in his tracks, then turned to take her face in his hands and kiss her again. Thoroughly. Sophie thought her lungs were going to burst from want of breathing but lack of remembering how. She was beginning to get used to the feeling of his lips on hers. It was both invigorating and petrifying.

When he released her, his grin was wolfish and wonderful. "Come on. We have a storm to catch up to, I'm starving, and I'm having an issue with my ailment."

She frowned as she followed after him. "Your ailment?"

He threw a smile back at her over his shoulder that should have been outlawed. "Yes. I'm running a fever. I think I'm totally 'hot for teacher.'"

She rolled her eyes at the complete cheesiness of his quoting the Van Halen song title, but her face betrayed her by flushing warm...again.

Chapter Four

Sophie never got tired of the Arizona lightning. It was power and grace rolled into one. It really was as Zane had said—nature's rock concert.

They had followed the storm sixty or so miles out of Phoenix to Roosevelt Lake. It was on the other side of the Superstition Mountains, roughly in the middle of nowhere. They had pulled off in a turnout by a bridge overlooking the lake, and for the longest time, neither one of them spoke. They just watched the lightning play across the sky while the thunder rolled from one end of the dark expanse to the other.

"Where are you from originally?" Sophie asked, finally breaking the silence. As a fan of the band, she should have known that, but she wasn't the stalker variety.

"Los Angeles," he replied. "But I hate it there. I live in Scottsdale when I'm not on tour."

She blinked rapidly, not having expected that he lived so close to her. "Do you really?"

He nodded and glanced over at her. "I love how it's warm here all year round, and I love the storms. I would have stayed at my condo while I was here, but we only had the one show. It's easier if I stay with the band."

"I live in Flagstaff."

"Beautiful place," he commented. "I ski there in the winter. Maybe I've seen you before and we passed right by one another."

"I think I probably would have remembered seeing you," she muttered.

He chuckled and reached for her hand. She continued to stare out at the light show while he toyed with her fingers. "Sophie, did you mean what you said earlier?" he asked. "That my music sounds how you feel inside?"

She looked over at him as he traced the lines in her palm. He didn't look up, and seemed almost self-conscious and vulnerable at that moment. She shifted so she was facing him. "Of course I meant it. Your music is amazing."

"What is it exactly? That you feel? What emotions does my music represent in you?"

Sophie smiled as she remembered the first time she'd ever heard a Shadows Rising song. It had been their first album, almost ten years ago. She'd been in college. "The first time I heard your band, I was studying for finals. I was burned out like never before. My roommate was into metal music. I wasn't so much at the time. I was studying classical, you know? But while I sat there, wracking my brain, trying to remember the square root of who knows what, questioning why I was putting myself through the torture at all, I heard this song. It was melodious and symphonic, with all the elements of beautiful music that I was in love with, but with this power behind it. Pounding drums, screaming guitar. It sounded how I felt. Chaotic, like I was losing control of everything in my world. For whatever reason, it made me feel better. I felt like, whoever had written that song must have felt the same insane, frazzled thing I was feeling, and that made it not so bad."

"That's the beauty of music. It's a universal language. A way of communicating with people you never meet. It touches people and lets them know that, no matter what they're feeling, they aren't alone. Someone else feels or has felt the same way. Even if the musician is a complete stranger, at that moment, to that person, he or she is a friend and a confidant, a companion. So no one, no matter how lonely, is ever truly alone."

She nodded in agreement and shifted to lean back against the car door, stretching her legs out across Zane's lap. He smiled and rested his hands on her knees. "I realized something else, though. After I was finished with finals and feeling like I was losing my mind, I still had this all-consuming desire to lose myself in your music, or in metal music in general. It had awakened this part of me I had never been allowed to be, and sometimes, I like to let that side of myself play when no one is looking."

He glanced at her and frowned. "What do you mean you

weren't allowed to be?"

She shrugged. "I've always been the practical one, the re-sponsible one. I've never been prone to fanciful daydreams. That was always my little sister's place. She was fanciful enough for a hundred of me. She's a ballet dancer and was always very creative, almost to a fault. She was wild and care-free and never thought anything through before she did it. My poor parents. They spent so much time pulling her out of the clouds and putting her back on firm ground. I didn't want them worrying about me, too. So I never did that rebellious thing most teenagers do. I was a good student. I studied hard. I had to show my sister a good example. Someone in the family needed to be level-headed. It was okay because I never had a desire to have crazy adventures like my sister did. I just wanted to teach. I wanted to inspire people, help people. And music has always been my passion, in any form."

"But there was always a rebel locked inside of you, dying to come out?" he teased.

Sophie smirked. "I'm not sure if I'd put it that way neces-sarily, but after I let myself be carried away by your music, it seemed like a good escape plan. Sometimes, work is stressful, and after a day of being inundated in Brahms and Handel, I just want to come home, drink a couple beers, lose myself in thundering metal, trade in my upright bass for a bass guitar, and jam away like I'm part of the band." She felt color creep into her cheeks at her admission. She'd never told anyone that. It had always been her little secret getaway.

Zane arched an eyebrow. "You play bass?"

"I play an upright bass. At home, by myself, I mess around with a bass guitar." She shrugged. "It's how I de-stress."

A slow, wicked grin curved his lips. "So it makes total sense that your smile made me hear a sexy bass line. That's amazing. I feel like I had a premonition. Do you know how to play all our songs?"

"Of course." She laughed, and he joined her.

He reached over and tucked a strand of her hair behind her ear. "Sophie, there's nothing wrong with having a little bit of a wild side. You don't need to hide it like it's a bad secret."

"But there's no place for it in my life. There's no point to it. I like my life. Maybe it seems boring to everyone else, but it's stable. It's safe."

"You can't always be afraid to take a risk every now and then, to taste and savor life instead of only doing what you need to survive. Life shouldn't be about survival, Sophie. Life should be about living."

She crossed her arms over her chest and fixed him with a pointed look. "Oh, yeah? Well, tell me, how come you, being someone who is constantly 'tasting' life, became so over-whelmed by it that you lost the line between musician and ce-lebrity and suddenly couldn't create anymore?" All traces of teasing left his face and he frowned, averting his eyes. "Be-cause it was too much, right? Too much stimuli. Too much life. There was no stability. And how come you, someone who is surrounded by beauty and creative freedom, somehow found me—grounded, stable, ordinary me—fascinating from the stage? What was it about me that caught your attention?"

He sighed. "Everywhere I looked, people were rocking out, head-banging, moshing, crowd-surfing, the way they always do. Women were dressed sexy or gothic, doing their best to get the attention of anything male that was onstage or off. It was the same thing I see every night. And then there was you. You were in jeans and a T-shirt. You weren't waving your arms or screaming at the top of your lungs. Not that I don't appreciate my fans' enthusiasm. I do. But, it all starts to blur together after a while. With you, there was this subtle, gentle light, like I said before. You were stripped down. Like an acoustic version of a metal song. And I felt like, in that ocean of people, you were really *appreciating* my music. Not just enjoying the sound and the beat, but you somehow heard all aspects of it. And when I looked at you, all the chaos, the stuff that was bombarding my mind, fell away and I could hear my music again." He absently trailed one hand up and down the length of her shin.

The corner of Sophie's lips lifted in a wry smile. "So, the simple woman escapes into metal music so she can feel wild and free in the confines of her own home, and the metal mu-sician seeks the company of a simple woman so all of the noise surrounding him disappears for a while. That's what I call an interesting conundrum."

He met her gaze, his eyes soft and warm. "I don't call that a conundrum, Sophie."

"What do you call it then?"

He reached over and cupped her cheek in his hand, feathering his thumb back and forth over her skin. "I call that perfect balance." He leaned closer, invading her space in the most intoxicating way.

Sophie let out a soft sigh, and her eyelids fluttered closed as his lips descended onto hers. She found absolutely no reason why she should try and push him away, or stop him from kissing her. Maybe it was foolish considering their worlds would never again collide after tonight, but what he said about them balancing one another seemed strangely true—at least it did at that moment. That squelched wild side that only came out in her living room during the evening hours was closer to the surface around him. She found herself wanting to let go a little, wanting to sample his rootless abandon. How many other opportunities would she get to run off into the night and kiss a rock star?

Maybe he was right about one thing. Safe wasn't always the only option. She was entitled to at least one adventure. So this would be hers. She couldn't let that side of herself out around anyone else. Everyone else in her life would think she'd lost her mind. But Zane was different. Everything about him and his life was the complete opposite of hers. But in this little window of time that they were together, he craved her stability and she craved his spontaneity. And she craved his touch and his kisses. For now, that was fine with her.

Zane and Sophie had migrated to the backseat. It was spacious, and there was a lot more leg room. The front seat was cramped, and—well, making out was awkward.

Zane felt like he was seventeen all over again, sitting in the backseat of a car, kissing a girl. It reminded him of a much more innocent and promising time in his life, when music was all he'd known and all he'd wanted. When celebrity status and red tape and the business end of it had never entered into his mind. He'd been full of optimism and dreams. And he'd somehow gotten lucky enough to receive everything he'd ever hoped for. He'd never imagined it would leave him feeling wanting. What did a person do when he became disillusioned with life?

Sophie sighed softly and snuggled against his shoulder. He glanced down at where she was resting. He had his legs stretched out across the seat, watching the lightning flicker farther and farther away, and she had curled up on his lap, against his chest. At some point, she'd dozed off. He didn't have the heart to wake her, and truth be told, he was reluctant to make the drive back to Phoenix.

The band had to leave tomorrow night. They had two shows in Southern California. One in San Diego and the other in Anaheim. He dreaded them, and that troubled him. He had never actually dreaded doing what he loved before. The fact that he was feeling that way now was disheartening and upsetting.

Was it as Sophie had said? Everything around him that made up the rock-star lifestyle had become too much? Did he crave the simplicity of a time when it had just been music and nothing else? Or was it something much more than that?

His heart told him the answer to that question as Sophie shifted slightly against him, nestling closer. His arms tightened around her, and he closed his eyes with a sigh. Maybe he was partly craving the simplicity of the past, but he also craved this. Companionship. Closeness. He was surrounded every day of his life by people, but he still felt empty. His music had sustained him thus far, had filled that hole inside of him, but now it seemed that it was no longer cutting it. He wanted something more than days full of travel and nights full of partying.

He wanted something real. Something solid and substantial in a world full of glitter and sparkle.

No wonder Sophie had intrigued him so much. She'd stood out in the crowd because she'd been different. She'd been subdued. It had been like a breath of fresh air. She loved his music, appreciated his talent, but was well grounded in the real world.

Her cousin had attacked him. *She* had attacked him—twice. But seeing her, talking with her, being with her, made him feel like he'd been on a whirling merry-go-round full of colors and sounds, and he was finally able to slow to a stop. He could take a full breath. He could think. He could hear his music. He hadn't felt anything even close to that since Shadows Rising had released their last album, and that had been three years ago.

His heart ached at the knowledge that he would have to say goodbye to her tomorrow. In a perfect world, he would ask her to go with him. She was so down to earth, so reality based, and he needed that so much in his world of fantasy and glamour.

He allowed himself to imagine what it might be like to have a normal relationship, a normal life. He had always wanted to be a musician. He had no desire to do anything else. It was his passion and his driving force. But instead of going home to an empty condo at the end of a tour, what might it be like to get off the plane, leave Zane Blake, keyboardist and composer of Shadows Rising, behind—hang him in the coat closet, so to speak—and just be Zane? Have someone come around the corner and greet him with a warm embrace and a passionate kiss?

Or better yet, what if he could take that persona off every night? Walk off the stage and into the arms of someone who made the world stop, like Sophie did? Someone who would talk with him at night, share quality conversation instead of booze-induced psychobabble. Someone who desired him, the man, and didn't only want his music, or his stage presence, or his blond hair blowing on a magazine cover.

He suddenly desired those things more than almost anything when they had never occurred to him before. Maybe he was getting old. Or maybe he was just getting tired. Tired of the endless party, the merry-go-round that never stopped.

He knew it would start up again once he was forced to say goodbye to Sophie. It was inevitable, and he despised it.

Chapter Five

The obnoxious blaring of a phone tore Sophie from her sleep and she instantly felt disoriented. She was hot and sticky like she had been sleeping in a sauna all night, and she had a horrible crick in her neck. Not to mention her back muscles felt like they may never function again.

Her bed moved. That was weird. She sat up, her back screaming in protest, and she blinked her eyes open in confusion. It took her a second to realize she was in the backseat of Lorraine's car, and she glanced over to see Zane Blake sitting next to her, looking just as confused and disheveled.

She had a small *holy crap!* moment before the previous night rushed back to her, along with a flush to her cheeks as she recalled him kissing her breathless and falling asleep in his arms.

"Oh my gosh," Zane grumbled as he ran his hand through his hair and tried to blink the sleep out of his eyes. "I have the worst case of taco neck ever."

"Taco neck?"

He glanced over at her. "Yeah, you know, where your neck is bent in half like a taco shell?" He rubbed at the side of his neck and groaned.

Sophie giggled. "At least it's not the same side I karate chopped."

He snorted. "Right, lucky me. Now the whole thing hurts equally." He smirked at Sophie and a sexy, soft light sparkled in his eyes. He leaned over and took her hand in his. "I like waking up to you." He smoothed some of her hair, which was undoubtedly a disaster, and kissed her gently on the lips.

Sophie's head swam and her heart did dip-and-dive moves. She didn't want to admit it out loud, but she really enjoyed waking up to him too.

His phone started blaring again and he scowled. He pulled back to fish around in his pocket and dug it out. "What?" he barked into it. Sophie watched as his expression changed from annoyance to shock. "Wait, Rhonda, slow down. I can't understand anything you just said... I'm fine. I'm with a girl." He glanced over at Sophie and she could have sworn she saw his cheeks turn pink. Then, his eyes bulged. "She *what?* Why?"

Sophie arched her eyebrows and waited while he spoke frantically with his band mate for a second before ending the call and staring straight in front of him like he had been kicked in the head. Finally, he expelled a forceful breath and raked his fingers through his hair.

"Kate just quit the band," he stated.

Sophie jolted. "What?" she exclaimed.

He looked over at her and shook his head slowly. "She was acting all weird last night after the show. Irritable and agitated. Apparently, she found out she's pregnant, and she just up and quit last night. Said she didn't want to raise a child on the road." The shocked look in his eyes slowly started to transform into panic. "I have no idea what we're going to do. She's left us in a lurch. Badly. We have a show tomorrow. Why couldn't she wait until the tour was over? It's not like she's going to deliver tomorrow."

Sophie climbed over the seat to the front and buckled in. She rolled down the window, since it was stifling hot in the car, and turned the key in the ignition. "Which hotel are you staying at? I'll take you back."

He climbed over the seat as well and plopped into the passenger seat with absolutely no grace whatsoever. "We're at the Four Seasons Resort in Scottsdale."

Sophie rifled around in her purse until she found her cell phone, then tossed it into Zane's lap. "Do me a favor. Text message Lorraine and tell her I'll come and pick her up later." She guided the car back out onto the road, relishing the feeling of the desert air blowing in her face and cooling her down. The monsoon season made everything humid and unbearable. Sleeping cuddled up on a person all night long with the windows rolled up had made her feel like her clothes were stuck to her skin. Not that she minded, really. It wasn't as if sleeping next to Zane had been a trial.

She sighed and rested her elbow on the window and her head in her hand while she steered with the other. This was a sucky way to have to say goodbye to Zane, but what did she expect? This was his life, his job. It wasn't like he could stay in the car and neck with her forever, as appealing as that option was to her.

She'd had her one night of adventure, and she'd gotten a wonderful memory out of it—much more than someone like she ever would have imagined for herself. She would be happy with that. He would go on to dazzle crowds every night, and she would go on to teach bored high schoolers. Their paths had crossed for a brief time, and they had both offered the other something important. That was all it could ever be, and she knew that.

But it still sucked.

Rhonda was a disaster. It was obvious she had been crying most of the night, and her eyeliner had run tracks down her cheeks. She looked like a bad version of Gene Simmons in his KISS makeup.

The other band members looked just as haggard and shell-shocked. Sophie felt awkward standing there as Rhonda continued to scream in hysteria. This wasn't her business in any way, shape, or form, but Zane refused to let go of her hand. He'd had it in a death grip ever since they'd gotten to the hotel. She'd tried to drop him off, but he'd had none of that. Told her that there was no way he was going to just wave goodbye like she'd been a chauffeur.

She'd tried to leave a couple of times, feeling out of place and like she was intruding, but every time she even remotely tugged her hand in a direction away from him, he shot her a warning glower that let her know he meant business. She didn't know why he was so adamant about her continued presence, but despite the uncomfortable situation, the fact that he wanted her there warmed her.

"I don't know what we're going to do," Rhonda continued to wail. "We're gonna have to cancel the tour! This is horrible!"

"We can't cancel the tour!" Billy exclaimed. "We have, like, six sold-out shows! First Zane loses him mind, and now this!"

"Thanks," Zane grumbled. "She seriously just bailed? She wouldn't even talk to you guys about it?"

Rhonda shook her head. "She just made an announcement that she was quitting. We tried to talk her into staying for the rest of the tour, but she said that it would be too much stress. She wanted to go home and be with her husband and...become a housewife or something. Who knows? All I know is that she screwed us big time."

"We need a new bass player, stat!" Matt interjected.

There was a small pause in the conversation before Sophie felt Zane's fingers tighten on hers ever so slightly. She had just enough time to feel impending doom before he turned to her—with this crazed look in his eyes—and shouted, "Wait! Sophie plays bass!"

Her heart crashed against her ribcage. "*What*?" she screeched. She tried to yank her hand out of his grasp, but he held on tighter. "Are you out of your mind?"

"You said you knew all our songs!"

All the band members' eyes riveted on her, and she wanted to turn and run as fast as she possibly could away from this bizarre situation. "So, what is that supposed to mean? Get a guitar tech to stand in! That's his job!"

Zane glanced back at the others over his shoulder.

"Dan has salmonella, actually," Matt supplied. "He's toast for at least another three days, doctor's orders. He has to stay on the bus, close to the bathroom or a bucket."

"Salmonella?" Sophie cried.

Zane turned back to her and clutched her hand with even more desperation. "Sophie, please."

"No way!" She finally managed to detach herself from Zane and stumbled backwards. "You are all insane! I'm a teacher!"

"Yeah, you teach *music*," Zane continued. "And you play the bass!"

"I play the *upright* bass!"

"A bass is a bass!" He fixed her with a pointed look. "And you told me that you play the bass guitar at home when no one's looking. And you play *our songs*."

Sophie felt her cheeks burn at him announcing that information to the room. She folded her arms across her chest and glared at him, feeling slightly betrayed.

"Please, Sophie," he begged.

"No freaking way, you absurd lunatic."

"Only a teacher would say it that way," Billy mumbled.

"Sophie," Zane implored, taking a step closer to her. "Listen to me. I wouldn't ask you if there was some other foreseeable option, but this is so last minute, and such bad timing all the way around. We only need someone for two shows. Just until Dan gets well."

She started to feel her chest constricting, and the veins in her forehead pounded as if they were going to explode. "You guys are musicians! You mean to tell me you don't know *anyone else* who can do this? Look at me, Zane! I'm not exactly rock-star material here!"

He frowned slightly. "Do you have stage fright? You shouldn't. You teach music, so that must mean you've played in front of people."

She snorted. "Yeah, in a big orchestra, playing freaking Beethoven or something. Not a lone bass player in a *metal band*. I'd have the stage presence of a doorknob!"

"Who cares if you have any stage presence?" Matt shouted suddenly. "Just stand there and pluck the strings! Stand behind the amp for all I care. Just play! Come on, lady, how many people would kill to be a rock star for a day? You're seriously going to stand here and leave us in the lurch when we're offering you an opportunity of a lifetime?"

"Dude." Zane turned to his band mate and positioned himself between Matt and Sophie. "Chill the hell out. I'm pretty sure screaming at her is not going to produce desired results. Not to mention, I don't like it."

"Well excuuuuse me," Matt mocked. "Didn't mean to *offend* you, Mr. High and Mighty. Forgive me if I'm a little angered over the sudden turn of events and lack of respect for all band members involved. And forgive me if I'm slightly annoyed at the fact that we have a *bass player* standing here acting like a wuss about something anyone else would be crapping their pants to do!"

"Matt!" Rhonda exclaimed.

Zane bristled and stabbed his finger at Matt. "You are so out of line right now. Keep going. I dare you."

"Who died and made you leader of the band all of a sudden?" Matt continued. "Last time I checked, you couldn't even write anything anymore. What happened? You get a good lay and suddenly all your creativity comes back?"

Zane lunged at Matt, but Rhonda shrieked and jumped in the middle. "You guys, stop it!" she cried. "What is the matter with you?"

Sophie rolled her eyes and strode over to the squabbling men. She grabbed Zane's arm and hauled him away from Matt, then shoved herself between them like Rhonda had done. "Oh my gosh!" she shouted. "How old are you two? Fifteen?" She turned to Zane, whose face was flushed with anger. She circled his wrist with her fingers until he looked at her. "I appreciate your defense, but I told you, I don't need someone to fight my battles for me. I'm very adept at defending myself." With that, she turned, faced Matt, and slapped him across the face hard enough that the crack echoed through the room.

Rhonda gasped and covered her mouth with her hands while Matt stumbled back in surprise and shook his head, his hand flying to his cheek. When he recovered, he stared at Sophie with shock.

"I know puberty is a rough time period, but one day, you'll be a man. Maybe. If you're lucky and pull your head out of your butt. Until then, do not talk about me like I'm not in the room, do not yell at me, and *do not* run your mouth like a testosterone-filled teenager on steroids when you have no idea what you're talking about. I have high school boys for students who are better behaved than you, Mr. Fancy-Pants Rock Star, and I have news for you. Being a bully and acting all tough and bad may get you what you want in this world, but in the real one, we have something called respect. And the fastest way to get me to *not* do what you want is to be disrespectful. So, what's going to happen right now is, you're going to apologize to me. Sincerely. Otherwise, you can take your dilemma and cram it where the sun doesn't shine."

There was a moment of complete and utter silence where everyone in the room just stared at her. She put her hands on her hips and waited.

Matt glanced around at all of his band mates, cleared his throat, hunched his shoulders like a chastised child, and stuffed his hands in his pockets. He looked up at Sophie and sighed. "I'm sorry. That was totally douche-baggy of me. I'm just a little stressed out. But that's no excuse for the crap I said."

Sophie nodded curtly and leaned closer to him. "And for the record, if Zane had done with me what you said he did, not only would he have his creativity back, but he'd have so much music oozing out of him he'd be able to play all the instruments himself and you'd all be out of a job. So, until you see that happen, watch your mouth."

There was another moment of total silence, and Sophie turned to see Zane staring at her with his jaw practically on the floor. Heat flooded her face as her anger dissipated.

He reached out to take her hand. "Here, let's go talk in the hall for a second." He pulled her out of the room and turned to face her when the door clicked shut. "Holy crap," he muttered.

She shrugged and bit her lip to stop a smile. "I told you I was good at defending myself."

"I guess...geez."

She giggled.

He sighed and ran his hands down her shoulders. "Sophie, I know this is weird, and last minute, and probably terrifying, but we really need your help. *I* need your help."

She looked up into his green eyes and saw only sincerity and a hint of desperation.

"I know Matt was being an idiot. He's always being an idiot. He doesn't know when to shut up."

She waved her hand. "Matt isn't an issue. He's a child. I deal with those every day. What's disconcerting to me is the fact that, sure, okay, I know how to play the bass and I have done so in public and at home and would probably be fine so long as I was given ample time to rehearse the set list, but, Zane, I don't know the first thing about being a rock star. About being a *performer*."

He chuckled and cradled her face in his hands. "Sophie, if you harness a fraction of the passion you displayed in that hotel room, you'll knock everybody's socks off. Just pretend everyone in the audience really pissed you off."

She laughed in spite of herself, but a wave of unease washed over her. "But I don't look remotely close to how a rock star is supposed to look. I'm just me. Just—"

"Don't you dare say boring. Rhonda can help you with your wardrobe if you want to look a bit more edgy. Otherwise, don't worry about it. You're so much more beautiful than you give yourself credit for."

Her heart melted and surrendered even while her rational mind was still screaming that she was the world's biggest idiot for considering this insane thing. She heaved a sigh. Apparently, her "one night of adventure" was like a runaway train with no tracks and no emergency brake. "I have to call the school. I have some personal time I can take."

His eyes lit up. "So, you'll do it?"

She fixed him with a stern expression. "Two shows." She held up her first two fingers for emphasis. "Just until your guitar tech is better. That's all."

He let out a whoop of elation and wrapped her up in his arms. "Thank you, Sophie. You have no idea what this means to me."

She closed her eyes and let his warmth permeate her. His arms were strong and steady, keeping her stable, but gentle, offering comfort. Oh man. She was so totally screwed.

"I have to take Lorraine's car back to her. This is going to be fun to try and explain."

"I'll go with you."

She smiled up at him. "Thanks. When is this first show I have to do?"

"Tomorrow night. In San Diego. We leave tonight."

She nodded. "As soon as we get back from this little chore, I'm going to need the set list, and I'm going to have you go over some of the songs with me so I know for sure what I'm doing."

"Of course." He started to open the hotel room door again, but then stopped and turned back to her with an arched eyebrow and a smirk. "All instruments at once, huh?"

A horrible wave of heat, worse than any she'd experienced since meeting him—and there had been a lot—spread over her face and neck, but to her credit, she didn't look down like she wanted to. She stood her ground and lifted her chin a notch. "Oh, you have no idea."

His eyebrows shot up so high they almost touched his hairline. He chuckled and slipped his arm around her waist, pulling her up against him and lowering his lips to hers. "You know that storm we watched last night?" he whispered. At her breathless nod, he nuzzled his lips against her neck and nipped at her earlobe. "That monsoon has nothing on you, baby."

She grinned. That may be the best thing anyone had ever said to her. When he pulled back, his eyes were full of warmth that set every part of her on fire. She could get used to him looking at her like that. Just like she could get used to him kissing her. She could get used to a lot of things...

Yeah, she was totally, totally screwed.

Chapter Six

Sophie stared at her reflection in the mirror for so long she started to lose concept of time. She kept thinking that, if she stared hard enough, she would see traces of herself, but she didn't. Like, not even one.

"Do you like it?" Rhonda asked as she finished with her hair.

The hair wasn't so bad. She could deal with the hair. All Rhonda had done was flat-iron it, put in some mud, or wax, or paste, whatever it was, and tousle it all up like she had a stylish case of bedhead. That was fine. It was the outfit she had picked for her and the makeup that was making her feel woozy. She'd stuck her in a black miniskirt, of all things, with red and black-striped tights and black combat boots. On top she was wearing a black tank top with a tight black fishnet shirt over it. Sophie could see Rhonda getting away with wearing it, but she felt completely exposed and completely ridiculous. Not to mention the heavy black eyeliner Rhonda had caked around her eyes and the bright red lipstick.

But Rhonda had been exceedingly nice to her, so she didn't want to hurt her feelings. She forced a meager smile. "I don't even look like me."

Rhonda grinned. "You'll be fine tonight, Sophie. Don't worry about it. You did awesome during sound check."

Sophie glanced at herself in the mirror again, and her chest started to feel really tight. She swallowed hard and fought a wave of dizziness.

Rhonda must have sensed her distress, because she put her hands on her shoulders in a gesture of comfort. "Do you want me to go get Zane?"

Sophie bobbed her head and felt tears burning her eyes. What was she doing here? This was ten kinds of crazy. In the last forty-eight hours, she had randomly accosted her favorite rock star, had run away with him into the night, made out with him in the back of a car, and decided to play substitute bass player for two nights at two sold-out heavy metal shows! She'd had to break that news to her cousin, which had been nothing short of WWIII, then get on a bus with a bunch of strangers and go to San Diego, where she'd been given a crash course in Shadows Rising songs. She'd practiced until her fingers were raw and she felt okay about the music, but this sudden disappearance of her own self was highly unsettling. This wasn't her. She didn't do things like this. She didn't *wear* things like this. She felt as if she had lost all traces of her personality in a matter of moments and had been replaced with some other version.

Zane entered the dressing room at that moment and she stood, then turned to face him.

"Whoa, look at you," he murmured, but it wasn't necessarily an enthusiastic response.

She tried to say something, but all that came out of her mouth was a shaky, wheezy sounding exhale. Her chest tightened even more, and the tears hovered right on her eyelashes.

Zane looked at her in confusion and concern and took her hands in his. "Are you all right?"

Again, she tried to speak, and again, all that came out was the same strangled sound. Her heart started to pound, and she could feel the blood thrumming in her ears.

"Sophie, I think maybe you need to inhale," Zane said.

She shook her head and sucked in a gasping breath of air. It hurt, and didn't feel like it was enough.

"Are you going to pass out?" he asked, his face etched with worry. "You gonna puke?"

She looked at what he was wearing. He looked gorgeous. Surprise, surprise. He always looked gorgeous. He was in a gray shirt with some skulls and whatnot all over it and a pair of black jeans with chains hanging from his left pocket. He looked normal, like himself. She, on the other hand...

"I don't even know who I am right now," she finally managed to rasp out. "What am I doing here?"

He frowned. "What do you mean? Sophie..."

"Look at me!" she shouted. "I look like some kind of

whacked-out pirate! This is not me! Who is this person? I can't handle this! I don't belong here!" She noted the hysteria in her voice and wondered where her rational mind had gone.

"Sophie!" Zane reached up and took her face in his hands. "Calm down, look at me."

She did so, and his lovely green eyes gave her a small measure of peace.

"This *is* you, Sophie. Just a different version of you."

She shook her head. "No! *This* is not me!" She indicated her abhorrent wardrobe. "Seriously, I feel like a doll. How am I supposed to go out on stage and do anything productive if I feel like a stranger in my own body? I'm not supposed to be edgy. I've never been edgy." The tears that had been threatening succeeded in cascading down her cheeks. "I'm boring, remember? I'm plain! I'm uninteresting and average. What am I even doing here? I'm going to have a heart attack!" She dissolved into soft sobs, hating her tirade of girlish insanity, but she felt more out of her element and out of control in that moment than she had in her entire life.

Zane's arms came around her, and he enveloped her in his comforting embrace. "How many times do I have to tell you that you are not boring?" he whispered, feathering kisses across the top of her head. "You've never been boring and you're never going to be. Although, I agree with you on the outfit. It's terrible." He took her by the shoulders and pulled away enough to wipe her tears away. "You look like some kind of gothic sailor vampire."

Sophie gave a watery laugh and wiped at her eyes.

Zane chuckled. "I love Rhonda like my own sister, and she means well, but she doesn't always realize that what she can wear, not everyone else can wear. Do you have your suitcase with you?"

"I don't have a suitcase, Zane. I was only driving down for one day to see the concert. All I brought was a backpack with a few essentials just in case. I need to hit a freaking store at some point. At any rate, it's over there." She pointed to the corner of the room.

He went over to her bag, rummaged through it for a minute, then came back with her jeans. "Put these on. I won't look." He winked at her and went back to her bag.

She smiled at his gentlemanly gesture, yanked off the

combat boots and the hideous tights, then discarded the miniskirt and tugged on her faded pair of jeans. She sighed in relief at the familiar comfort. "Well, I feel half like myself," she stated.

He came back with a black shirt in his hand that he set aside. Then he reached out and lifted the black fishnet over her head. Her breath caught at the subtly intimate action, and when his hands came back down to toy with the hem of the tank top as well, electricity arced between them and made the room feel sweltering.

"You want me to turn around again?" he murmured.

She licked her suddenly dry lips, loving the green fire burning in his eyes. She shook her head. "It's okay, I have a bra on. Just like a bikini, right?"

Something dangerous flashed over his features, but he said nothing else. With painful slowness, he pulled the tank top off also. He flung it on the floor, and his fingers brushed across the bare skin of her torso for a moment. She sucked in her breath at the velvet-soft contact. His eyes grazed her in a heated way before he reached over to grab the shirt he had chosen for her to wear.

When he had pulled it over her head, she glanced down to see it was an old Pantera T-shirt she sometimes slept in. She frowned. "Are you serious? Just a plain old T-shirt?"

He smiled as he freed her hair from the collar of the shirt. "Rock and roll is all about music and attitude. It shouldn't be about fashion or frills. There is nothing more rock and roll than a band shirt and a faded pair of blue jeans." His gaze softened. "Maybe that was what caught my attention from the stage. Seeing you was like looking at my roots. Just plain ol' rock and roll, before all the hoopla." He stepped back to look her over and grinned. "There's my girl."

Tingles fizzled throughout her body at being called *his girl*, and she turned to look at herself. She sighed in relief at the more familiar reflection. She wiped off the lipstick but decided the eyeliner could stay, and she messed her hair up a little bit more. That was better. Rocker Sophie. Slightly edgy Sophie. But still Sophie. Some normalcy seeped back into her, more of her methodical mind and less of the crazed, panic-attack-waiting-to-happen side.

She turned back to Zane, who was smiling softly at her.

He was all confident poise and beauty. All raw talent and bad-boy rock star. But he had such a gentle, kind heart. She could understand how the rock-star life had taken over to the point where he hadn't been able to create anymore. In only a matter of a few short moments, she felt like she had been robbed of her identity by a bad choice of clothing. How much worse must it be to have all the pressures of stardom slowly creep in and suffocate all the parts of the life that you had originally fallen in love with? No wonder Zane had started to feel so out of control. He had lost touch with himself, with the whole reason he loved to do what he did.

She sighed and slipped her arms around his waist. He held her tight and she closed her eyes, resting her cheek on his chest and listening to the rhythm of his heartbeat.

"You'll do fine, Sophie," he murmured.

She looked up at him and shook her head. "I'm not worried about that. I'll muddle through somehow."

A small frown creased his brow. "Then what is it?"

She slid her palms up his chest and across his shoulders, smoothing the fabric of his shirt and studying the texture of his muscles. "Zane, what was it that originally made you love music so much? What made you want to do this so badly?"

"It's always been in me, the sounds and the notes, even before I knew what they were. I wouldn't know what to do with myself if it wasn't there... It's who I am. Without it, I would be lost. I *was* lost."

She smiled softly. "Then maybe you need to take off the black miniskirt and the red lipstick too." She giggled at his expression. "Get back to your roots, like you said. Put on a pair of blue jeans and a band shirt, metaphorically speaking."

He stared at her for several seconds with a look of contemplation on his face before a soft smile curved his lips. "Find myself and just forget all the rest."

She nodded and studied his wonderful face. She'd never in her wildest dreams imagined she'd be here right now, with him, about to do what she was about to do. She still kept expecting to roll over and wake up.

She couldn't quite describe the look he gave her. But it was full of sincere warmth, gentleness, and something smoldering that made her heart flop around in her chest. He took her hand and raised it to press a tender kiss to the inside of her wrist. He continued up her arm until he got to her elbow. Then he placed it around his neck and aligned his body with hers. Something passed between them. Something more intense and more intimate than anything they had shared thus far.

Sophie lost herself in his eyes and raised her lips to meet his. His kiss was soft and slow, and when his tongue delved in her mouth to deepen it, she felt her knees grow weak, as cliché as that was. She surrendered to the kiss, handing herself over to him, allowing him to do what he would. Never in her life had anyone kissed her the way Zane did, and she knew it was going to ruin her for any other man. That was only one of the many dilemmas she had discovered since meeting him.

He kissed her like she was the only woman who had ever existed in the world, or at least in his world. It was one of her weaknesses when it came to Zane. He didn't make her feel like a groupie, or like one of the many. He made her feel special, like he cherished her just for being who she was. He was the only person who had ever made her feel that way.

She didn't know if it was hero worship or what. All she knew was that she liked it. It was nice to feel like something extraordinary for a change instead of just like "Sophie."

He reached up to tangle his fingers in her hair, monopolizing her mouth, claiming her in a way that made her dizzy. Zane was the type of person who went after what he wanted, and it sure seemed like he wanted a lot of her lately.

He backed her up against the makeup counter, then reached down to take hold of her hips, never breaking contact with her mouth. He lifted her so that she was sitting on the counter and wrapped her legs around his waist. A small groan escaped Sophie before she could sensor it, and she felt him smile against her lips.

She pulled him close, and he trailed hot kisses along her jaw and neck before returning to her mouth. He tugged on her hair enough to make her suck her breath in, and his chuckle was low, wicked, and wonderful.

"Guys, we go on in ten—heyyohh! My bad."

Rhonda's voice yanked them from their passion-induced personal moment, and Zane expelled a slow breath, resting his forehead against Sophie's. Sophie gave a soft, breathy laugh and played with the ends of his hair for a second, trying to get her heartbeat under control. When she had succeeded, she met his gaze, smiled, and touched his face tenderly. She loved the hard line of his jaw, his straight nose, full lips, and searing green eyes. She loved the feel of his skin against hers, and she particularly loved the way he touched her—assertive, yet gentle, and every caress left her aching for more of him. Not just out of lust, but because every time he showed her a little more of his heart, it blinded her with its radiant light. He was more than a performer, more even than a musician. He was addictive.

She sighed softly. "What do you say, music man? Wanna go put on a show?"

His grin dazzled her and he nodded, then kissed her one more time. He moved back enough for her to be able to get down off the counter, and she glanced at Rhonda, who was pretending to be invisible, she imagined.

When Rhonda felt it was safe to look at them again, she frowned, and her expression reflected disappointment. "Oh, you changed. You didn't like my outfit?"

"There's only one front woman in this band," Zane said before Sophie could formulate a response. "Why would you want to upstage yourself, beautiful? You're the only one who should be commanding such attention." He kissed her chastely on the forehead, and Rhonda smiled up at him in adoration.

Sophie smothered her grin and followed Zane and Rhonda out the door. Her stomach did somersaults in anticipation of what she was about to do. Oh well—now or never.

Sophie Gilkins—teacher, musician...rock star. Why not?

Here went nothing.

Chapter Seven

As he took his place at his keyboard and waited while their intro music played, Zane wondered if he was actually more nervous than Sophie. She was a no-nonsense, get-the-job-done type of person. His stomach felt like it had decided to buy out real estate in his windpipe. He hadn't had jitters this bad since the first time he'd performed in front of an audience.

He knew she would do fine. She'd played wonderfully at sound check, and he wasn't worried about the band. Even if she sucked in the stage presence department, the rest of the members could compensate.

It made him analyze his nerves a little more, look at the situation a little closer, and as he did, he realized it wasn't adrenaline from fear he was feeling. It was excitement. He wasn't afraid that Sophie wasn't going to do a good job. He was excited because he got to share his world with her, his life. They were going to perform together, perform songs *he* had composed. It was a sharing of his heart, and it seemed so intimate to him.

As the lights came up and the opening guitar riff of their first song played, Zane's heart lurched for one suffocating second before the rest of the band launched into it. The crowd screamed, and Zane glanced over at Sophie. She was situated on the far side of the stage, and he could tell she was playing because he could hear the bass line. Other than that, she may as well have been a statue. He could barely see her fingers moving.

He smiled to himself, and his heart went out to her for a moment. This had to be the last thing she really wanted to be doing. She was a teacher, not a performer. She was only doing this to help him out of a jam. He felt badly for forcing her into it. At least she was playing correctly, and she was no longer in that freakish outfit. No doubt that wouldn't have helped her feel comfortable.

Tearing his gaze away from Sophie and doing his best not to think about that kiss they had shared in the dressing room, Zane turned his attention back to his keyboards and lost himself in his music and in his nightly routine.

What am I doing here? Oh, right. Attempting not to crap my pants.

Sophie tried to block out the sound of the crowd while she concentrated on where her fingers were going.

Just play the bass... Play the bass. Half a song down. A hundred thousand more to go.

That's about how it felt. It was like time had slowed down. Either that or she had somehow managed to cross into another dimension and was living in both of them simultaneously. Because she felt like she was outside of her body watching what was going on.

And holy cow, did she ever suck.

The music was all right. She wasn't having trouble with that. But she felt like a cigar-store Indian, and she knew she had about as much personality as one. Something needed to be done about this. She couldn't play the entire show this way. Not only would people start to wonder if she was actually capable of movement, but she'd be walking like the Tin Man afterward because all her joints would have locked up.

After the first song was over, Rhonda greeted the audience with enthusiasm and was met with roaring screams and applause in response. Sophie forced herself to stand up straight, to shift positions a bit. Her back was already angry at her. She glanced over at Zane, who was looking back at her as if to ask her the silent question, *Are you going to die?* That's probably what she looked like. Eyes bulging like the deer about to bounce up and over somebody's Ford Taurus. And yes, the vision really was *that* detailed that she knew what kind of car it was.

She glanced at all of the other band members. With the exception of Rhonda, who was still talking to the audience, they were all looking at her with the same expression. Like they feared she was going to bolt and they were all going to have to make a mad dash to block the exit doors.

She took a small peek at the crowd, and her stomach dropped down to the South Pole. Her heart started to beat way too fast, and her head spun in a dizzying manner that made her feel somewhat nauseous. *Get a grip, Sophie. This is not the first time you have ever been on stage.*

No, she argued with herself. *But this is the first time you've ever played the bass guitar as a stand-in for your favorite band...after making out with the keyboard player, AKA your idol!*

Her stomach plummeted again and she looked around somewhat wildly until her gaze met and held Matt's. He raised an eyebrow in question, and she yanked the guitar off as she all but ran off the side of the stage to the wings.

Matt followed, looking somewhat panicked. "What are you doing? Are you okay?"

"I need something strong, ASAP."

He frowned. "Something strong?"

"Yeah! Whiskey! Vodka! Friggin' Wild Turkey! I don't care what it is! You're a rock star. I know you guys have to have something handy!" The drum tech handed her a bottle of Southern Comfort and muttered something about how Wild Turkey *was* whiskey. She ignored him, sighed in relief, and unscrewed the top. "Thank goodness. Now I know why you people all drink so much." She chugged back about a shot's worth, and the fiery, much-too-sweet liquid burned a path down her asphyxiating throat and into her gyrating stomach.

Matt chuckled. "Liquid courage at its finest."

She downed one more slug and made a face, wiping her mouth with the back of her hand. "I don't need courage. I need a psychiatrist. This is insane." She handed the bottle back to the drum tech and expelled a forceful breath.

"Better? Do you need me to get Zane?"

Why did everyone keep asking her that? "No, I do not need you to get Zane. I am a grown woman. I don't need a daddy or a bodyguard. I just needed a couple shots of something to kill the dancing gnome in my stomach." She squared her shoulders. "All right." She slipped the bass back on and faced the stage.

"You good?" he queried.

She gave a curt nod and tromped back out, determined to see the job through.

Zane and Rhonda looked slightly petrified when she glanced at them upon her return. Zane started toward her, but she held up her hand as she took her position.

Rhonda hurried over to her and slipped an arm around her shoulders. "Are you okay, sister?" she whispered in her ear.

Sophie nodded. "Better now. I needed a tiny *me* moment."

"You good to go on?"

She set her jaw and lifted her chin. "Let's do this thing." She strummed the strings on the bass to check the pitch, which drew random screaming from audience members.

Rhonda smiled and turned back to the crowd, keeping her arm around Sophie. She lifted the mike she held in her other hand. "All right, everybody, how about a little bit of action?" Screaming. "Maybe a little bit of pile-driving?" More screaming.

Sophie couldn't help but smile as the band, herself included, launched into one of their most famous songs, "Pile-driver." It was the first song she had heard from Shadows Rising, the one that had hooked her, and it made her chuckle because now it reminded her of what Lorraine had done to poor Zane only two nights ago.

As the last forty-eight hours replayed themselves through her mind at whirlwind speed, and mixed with the alcohol tingling its way through her veins, complete joy began to chase out the feelings of all-consuming terror she had just been feeling.

Look where you are right now! You're playing bass for Shadows Rising! You're playing on stage with Zane Blake! You are part of Shadows Rising right now!

She grinned as the jubilation took over, and she found the upper half of her body moving in time to the beat of the song. Not only that, but her legs had somehow managed to spread themselves into a power stance.

She closed her eyes and listened to the familiar song. She never would have thought all those years ago that she would one day be playing on stage in San Diego the exact same song that had first introduced her to metal, to Shadows Rising, to Zane and his amazing talent. What had happened to her life in the past two days?

A whole lot of stuff that you shouldn't take for granted.

Wasn't that the truth? So many people would be so envious of where she had managed to end up right now. She needed to soak up this moment and cherish it. Something like it may never come again.

As she returned from her meandering thoughts and the song winded to a close, she realized she was standing at the edge of the stage and her limbs felt loose and fluid, no longer stiff and awkward. She played the last few measures with ease, and the fans directly in front of her shouted, screamed, and reached out to her. On impulse, she leaned down to touch all of their hands. Something strange like electricity coursed through her veins. It was exhilarating. It was addictive.

As she moved back to where she had originally been standing, she stole a look up at Zane. The grin he shot her made her whole world explode like a fireworks display.

And in that moment, she realized, it wasn't the alcohol and the drugs and the fast living that was addictive, which was what she had always assumed before of people who did this as a job. It was this. This experience. This rush. Knowing *you* were the reason those four girls in the front row were screaming. Knowing *you* were so good at your craft that people wanted to learn your parts of the songs. This was the addictive thing. And once bitten, how did you ever get it out of your system?

She looked over at Zane again and, as she did so, he winked and blew her a kiss. Her heart tumbled around in her chest. Once bitten—or kissed—how did she get *him* out of her system?

Chapter Eight

Sophie sighed in bliss as she leaned back in the enormous tub in the master bathroom of her hotel suite. She was both exhausted and exhilarated and found the combination a strange kind of intoxicating.

She still had a little of that weird, out-of-body thing going on. Part of her couldn't believe that only an hour before, she had finished up playing a concert with Shadows Rising. But she had. And when Rhonda had introduced all the band members, and had announced her like she had always been part of it all, and when the crowd had cheered, something odd had happened inside of her. She'd liked it. A lot.

Safe, subdued, rational Sophie had totally gotten off on the rush of recognition. She had about as much of an idea about what to do with that as she did about what to do with Zane.

She liked him much more than was healthy. She knew that, yet she didn't care. She *liked* liking him. She liked being with him. She really liked kissing him. He was gentle and caring, thoughtful, but playful enough to make her lighten up a bit. Had she always been so serious? She'd never realized it before. In her quest to be the "responsible one" in her family, had she sacrificed all ability to let loose and have a good time? If so, no wonder Lorraine had always called her boring. That *was* boring. What good was she to anyone if all they ever saw of her was this staunch, predictable person who never ventured outside of her safe routine—except, of course, when she was by herself in her living room jamming away on a bass like a rock star?

Maybe Zane was right. Maybe she had been only been surviving her life. Tonight, on that stage, she had felt more alive than she ever had. Had she wasted thirty years being "safe"?

A knock sounded on her hotel room door and she jumped in surprise. "Just a second!" she called. She climbed out of the tub, toweled off, and slipped into the white hotel robe. She went to the door and opened it to see Zane standing there with two plastic bags and his gorgeous grin. She arched an eyebrow and glanced at the clock on the wall. The show had ended at eleven. It was now well past twelve-thirty.

"I know it's late," he said, "but that's kind of the way it goes around here. Rock musicians are mainly nocturnal. At any rate, I want to conduct an experiment."

Her raised eyebrow arched even higher. "That sounds ominous."

He chuckled, and warmth filled his eyes as he gazed at her robe-clad, wet-haired form. "It's nothing bad, I promise. Can I come in?"

Like she would actually deny him. She stepped aside, allowing him entry.

"Have you eaten anything yet?"

She shook her head as she closed the door. "That was next on my agenda after I got the stage sweat and cigarette smoke off my body."

He held up one of the bags. "Well, I got us some Chinese at this place that is apparently open till midnight, which was awesome." He held up the other bag. "And then I had to try and decide if you would rather have wine or beer. I figured wine would be more romantic and all, but then I remembered how you said you like to go home and knock back a couple of brewskies."

She grinned. "I'm definitely more of a beer girl."

"Do you like football too?" he teased.

"Of course I do." She eyeballed him in similar mischievous fashion. "You're not a Raiders fan, are you?"

He looked at her like she was nuts. "Uh, no, I live in Arizona. I'm a Cardinals fan."

She laughed. "All right, good. My test is finished. You passed. Go ahead and make yourself comfortable. I'm going to go put on some clothes."

"Or you could just wear that."

"I'm naked under here."

He fixed her with a smoldering look. "All the more reason. We could conduct another experiment…"

She shot him a playful scowl and practically ran out of the room before she took him up on his unspoken offer. He was incorrigible, and he made her want to act rebellious. That was another thing she totally didn't know what to do with. Apparently, she had a whole other person living inside of her that she had repressed all of these years. That person liked to try and surface when Zane was around.

Rhonda had loaned her some of her clothing, thank goodness, but she still needed to hit a mall or something tomorrow. She could deal with the black tank top and gray track pants to sleep in, but lord only knew what Rhonda would try to stick her in for the show tomorrow night if she didn't get herself a couple of outfits of her own. And she seriously needed some underwear. She'd only brought two pairs, and as it was, she'd had to wash out the ones she'd worn tonight in the bathroom sink.

After donning her sleepwear, she headed back out into the living room area where Zane had already unloaded all of the food. He was sitting on the floor at the coffee table, and the vision made her smile. For some reason, she could picture this being a nightly routine for her. She loved takeout, so she couldn't see herself getting tired of eating it, and her body and mind would adapt to a night schedule just like if she was working graveyard. So she wouldn't have to worry about gaining four hundred pounds from eating so late.

It would be nice to unwind with Zane every evening. Talk about the high and low points of the show, the crowd, the funny things that happened backstage. They could eat and laugh, make out, enjoy one another in companionable silence...

What am I thinking? She mentally slapped herself and told herself to get a grip. Why was she planning this out in some kind of long-term existence? She had one more show to play with the band, and then she would be back in Flagstaff and back to her own life. She was filling in to help out until the guitar tech got well enough to play. They weren't considering her for the next great bass player of Shadows Rising. That was ridiculous. Besides, she didn't want that anyway. She wanted to go back home to her routine and the stable life she had built for herself.

But even as she reprimanded her straying thoughts, her

heart felt heavy at the knowledge that, after tomorrow, it was all over.

As Sophie came out in her loaned PJs, makeup free, her hair damp from the bath she'd taken, Zane's heart leapt in a way he hadn't experienced since he'd been a teenager. It all looked so natural, everything—the food and the beer, her coming out in her pajamas to eat and talk with him after a long day. It was everything he had come to realize he craved.

A slice of normal life in the midst of all the chaos. Someone to unwind and share with after all the insanity of the shows.

It was her. It had to be her. She was the only person who had ever made him feel like everything worked. She fit. She balanced him in a way he had never expected. She was the missing piece.

He held his arms out to her as she sat down next to him, and she smiled as she snuggled against him. He held her and closed his eyes with a sigh.

"So, what's this experiment anyway?" she asked.

He pulled away enough to look down into her eyes. He brushed a wet strand of hair off her forehead and smiled. "It's done already. I already know the answer."

She frowned. "And that is?"

"You." He captured her lips with his, his body and heart aching for her, and aching at the knowledge that she would leave him in a little over twenty-four hours.

She laughed softly as she pulled away. "You certainly have a way with words, Zane Blake."

He grinned and they turned to their dinner, lapsing into conversation that spanned a wide array of subjects. They laughed, shared stories of their lives and their past, cuddled, kissed. It was the most perfect moment Zane had ever experienced. He saw his future in it, and in Sophie's eyes. All he had to do was find a way to make it all work out, and make her realize it was what she wanted too.

Although, part of him figured she knew already. She just had to admit it to herself.

Chapter Nine

Sophie sighed as the taxi dropped her off in front of her house. She felt like she'd been traveling forever, considering she'd had to fly from Los Angeles to Phoenix and then have a cab drive her to Flagstaff. Her bank account was a little bit fatter, since she'd actually been paid by the Shadows Rising business manager for her stand-in routine, and she had more luggage than when she had first arrived in Tempe, but she felt bedraggled and empty.

Her two-bedroom, two-bath house looked lonely for the first time ever. It was strange and, in all reality, kind of annoying. Her home had always been a place of solace and refuge. Now, because she'd spent four days with a rock star and his posse, it seemed lacking? What was up with that? Her whole life had been thrown out of balance.

The part that sucked the most was that, try as she might to be annoyed by the whole ordeal, she wasn't. She was sad. Sad to leave Zane and sad to leave the whole experience. So, she was manifesting it in annoyance so she could try and fool herself. Except, it wasn't working.

She thought of Zane's departing words. After one more show and another night spent unwinding with laughter, good conversation, and downtime in Zane's arms, he had stood at the airport with her and promised he would call her. Yeah, right. And then he'd told her that he would come and see her after the tour was over. Double yeah, right. As much as she wished that might actually happen, she knew he would forget about her in time. How could he not? She wasn't anything special.

Oh, Sophie, stop being such an idiot. You know you meant something to him, and Zane's not like that. Stop trying to turn him into a jerk just because it would be easier for you to deal with your dilemma if he was.

She scowled and refused to acknowledge that meddle-some voice that kept creeping into her thoughts. She was too tired to deal with *that* right now.

She made her way to the front door and let herself in. She flopped her backpack in the foyer and left it there, then went to her answering machine. She had three messages. Whoop-de-do. That's how significant she was in the grand scheme of life. She was gone for almost five days, and she got three messages.

The first one was from Lorraine. "Sophie, I still can*not* believe what you did to me. Sending me home while you stole my man and went running off with the band like some kind of skank groupie. I am so mad at you right now. I don't even know when I'll be ready to talk to you again, so just don't bother calling me for a while."

Sophie rolled her eyes and hit the delete button. Like not being able to talk to Lorraine was a real hardship.

The next message made her eyebrows shoot up because it was from Zane.

"Sophie, I wanted you to know how much you managed to change my life while you were here with me, for the bet-ter. I know you don't believe I'm going to contact you after the tour, but I will. I promise you. Good luck getting rid of me now."

She deleted that one also, as quick as she could, just be-cause it was easier to get on with her life if she pretended he didn't really give a crap. That and it was much easier to ig-nore the annoying voice in the back of her mind telling her that her place was with him instead of living a boring, pre-dictable existence twenty-four-seven.

The next message, to her shock, and to the dismay of the part of her that was in denial, was also from Zane.

"I hope you have a lovely evening, Sophie. I am thinking of you, and wish you were here with me. I've gotten spoiled having you around to talk with after the show...and I miss holding you...desperately."

She didn't erase that one. She couldn't. In fact, she played it one more time before she sank to the ground and fought tears. Something strange had happened since she'd met Zane. Some dormant part of her had awakened—the part of her that apparently liked rocking it on stage to a screaming crowd—and she didn't know how to go back to the life she had once known. How could she? Now that she had tasted that rush? Now that she had tasted Zane?

She propped her elbows on her knees and put her head in her hands. Her whole life, she had been in control. Now she felt anything but. Now, she felt...lonely.

What was she supposed to do with that? Especially when life went on and she was powerless to stop the inevitable progression of time?

Sophie felt out of sorts as she made her way down the hall toward her classroom. She'd given herself the "get back to work and back to your normal life" speech about a hundred times, but it didn't seem to be helping much. She felt dismal, and missed Zane, and hated herself for getting attached to him in the first place when she'd commanded herself not to. It seemed, as of late, she was having a very difficult time listening to her own common sense. That was not a problem she'd ever had before, and she didn't like it very much.

She pushed open the door with a sigh and jumped back in shock when hoots, hollers, and shouts from her students greeted her. She frowned and looked over at all of them as they cheered.

"Woohoo! Go, Ms. G!"

"Yeah, way to rock it, *Sophie Storm*!"

She blinked in bewilderment and went to set her things over on her desk. "What in the world are you all talking about?" she asked as she addressed her rambunctious students.

Elliott, a charismatic, talented boy who leaned toward the metal end of the music spectrum, laughed. "Are you serious? Like you don't know what we're talking about. Shadows friggin' Rising! How did you get *that* gig?"

She stared. "You know about that?" She wasn't quite sure if that was good or bad. She didn't think her school district would have an issue with it, but still.

"Dude, *everyone* knows about Sophie Storm!" Elliott's best friend and partner in crime, Aaron, shouted.

She frowned and put her hands on her hips. "Why do you keep calling me that?"

"That's what everyone is calling you!" Elliott cried. "You're all over YouTube and Facebook, and I even saw a clip of you on *Entertainment Tonight*!"

She felt the color drain out of her face. "Are you serious?" she squeaked.

"Well, yeah. Kate quitting the band caused a feeding frenzy in the media," Aaron said. "And now people want to know who this mysterious Sophie is that came out of nowhere and blew everyone's minds!" He made a very dramatic "exploding head" gesture with his hands and jumped up on his chair in enthusiasm.

"They've labeled you Sophie Storm," Julie, Elliott's girlfriend, supplied.

"Why?" She hated how completely meek and passive she sounded. She didn't like seeming pitiful or out of control in front of her classes, but...shoot. *Entertainment Tonight*?

"Because you're like a typhoon of rockness!" Aaron continued to perform, standing on his chair and doing some sort of Elvis hip-wiggle thing, which he followed up with some air guitar, a couple head bangs, and the rock-on sign with his tongue slithering out like a snake for good measure.

"Oh please," she muttered, trying to get some kind of grip on this situation before her face ignited and Aaron decided to start sacrificing pigeons or something. "Zane's a friend. I was trying to help him out." That was...basically right. "It's not like I'm part of the band now." She hated how her heart twisted in protest at her even saying those words. "They were in a bind. I just happened to be there..."

"You *know* Zane Blake?" Elliott screeched. "He's your *friend*?"

Her face burned, but she managed to nod. *Friend* was such a weak word for what she felt for Zane.

"I didn't know you played electric guitar, Ms. Gilkins!" Julie added.

Sophie smiled, and an overwhelming wave of joy surged through her at the thought that, for one second in time, she had actually been somebody. She bet Lorraine *really* wanted to kill her now. She'd never thought recognition would matter, but it did. Especially from her students. "Well, I don't tell you guys *all* my secrets," she teased. "Now, enough playing around." She pointed at Aaron. "Get down, Ozzy. We have work to do."

The students laughed, and she went over to grab her sheet music so she could begin the lesson. Her heart felt warm where it had been empty and aching only moments before, and she realized that, regardless of how everything ended up, she'd had an experience of a lifetime.

And she was grateful for her adventure.

Chapter Ten

Four months later

It was a day like any other. Just like they'd all been since she'd first returned to work and reality after her brief stint as stand-in rock star. She'd gotten back into her routine and went about her business as she always had, but she still hadn't been able to banish the small hole in her heart that had been there since she'd left Shadows Rising. It was like Zane had taken a little piece of her that she would never get back again. She didn't know what to do with that. Get used to it, she guessed.

While he had called her rather diligently for the first two months after her return to Flagstaff, she'd heard relatively little from him since their tour ended. Figured. She couldn't pretend that it didn't hurt. Even though she'd tried to prepare herself for this inevitability, it still sucked. Especially since they had gotten to know one another so much better over his telephone calls. Because of that, her feelings for him had only deepened instead of diminished.

"Get over it, Sophie," she muttered to herself as she made her way to her room for the after-school rehearsal of the fall concert. "It was a nice little reprieve from your predictable life. That's all. You knew this was going to happen, so deal with it and be happy your paths crossed at all."

She stepped into her classroom and was startled to see all of her students already in there. Usually it took them awhile to meander in after their last class when they did rehearsals like this.

"Ms. G!" Elliot shouted, jaunting over to her with Aaron and Julie in tow. "Come on, we have to go to the gym."

She blinked rapidly. "Why?"

He fixed her with a look. "The special assembly."

She frowned. "Special assembly? What are you talking about?"

He arched an eyebrow. "You know, the special after-school assembly everyone has been talking about for like a month now."

Was she losing her mind? Had she completely forgotten about an assembly and scheduled rehearsal on top of it? She searched her memory and couldn't place ever hearing about an assembly of any kind. "Elliott, I have no idea what you're talking about."

"Come on, Ms. Gilkins!" Julie interrupted. "We're going to miss it, and it's supposed to be really cool!"

Sophie's frown deepened. Julie was a pretty level-headed girl. If she was saying this assembly was real, maybe Sophie really had spaced it. "What is it even supposed to be?"

"Something to help the arts and music program. *Come on!*" Elliot insisted.

"Okay, okay, fine. Let's go to the gym." She followed her excited students to the gym, all the while wracking her brain about this mysterious assembly, and coming up short. She was so involved in her own thoughts that, when she walked through the double doors into the gym and was met by up-roarious cheering, she screamed and almost hit the roof she jumped so hard.

She looked over at the bleachers bursting with kids, teachers, and parents first, then slid her gaze over to the stage that had been erected in the middle of the basketball courts. Her heart did backflips and cartwheels as she spotted a very familiar tall, blond man making his way toward her with the biggest grin she had ever seen.

"Wh..." She swallowed hard and tried to remember how to verbalize. "What...what the hell?" she whispered.

Elliot and Julie exchanged surprised glances. "Holy crap, Ms. G just swore," he murmured.

Sophie was trembling when Zane approached her, and was thankful for his ever-present poise because she felt like she was going to poop her pants. He chuckled, which meant she must have looked as shocked as she felt.

He lowered his lips to her ear and whispered, "Hello again...Sophie Storm."

She felt heat flood her cheeks. Of course. If she wasn't in a perpetual state of red around Zane, he would think she was sick.

She reached out to place her fingertips lightly on his chest, to assure herself that he was real, that she wasn't dreaming. "What are you doing here?" she squeaked. As she looked past him, she could see the other band members tuning up on stage. She frowned. *What in blue blazes is going on?* She looked back up at Zane and her heart melted, much to her chagrin. He was just as beautiful as she remembered, and she turned into a blushing groupie around him.

He reached down and took her hands in his, never losing his smile. He was the picture of confidence, the picture of talent, the picture of the man of her dreams. "Sophie, I want to discuss something with you."

"Discuss? For starters, discuss what your band is doing in my gym!"

He chuckled. "We're putting on a show. It has been very difficult keeping it a secret from you, but I had some good help." He threw Elliott, Julie, and Aaron a wink.

Sophie frowned and turned to her students. "You all planned this behind my back?"

"I wanted it to be a surprise," Zane interrupted. "If you'd known ahead of time, you probably would have rationalized it until there was no juice left. This needed to be fueled by pure emotion, because only then are you honest with yourself. If anything, I have learned that about you over the last several months."

She would have protested, but she couldn't...because he was right. Plus, at that precise moment, he reached up and took her face in his hands, and she was lost. She had missed his touch, missed his presence, missed everything about him.

"All the proceeds from ticket sales tonight are going directly to the arts and music program here at your school."

She looked up at him and felt tears burn her eyes.

"In addition to that, I have an offer for you." He pointed to the stage. "Over there are three musicians ready to put on a rock concert, but we're minus a bass player. Now, we have Dan, the guitar tech, who is sufficient, but lacking in the stage presence department. Not to mention the fact that all of our fans keep asking for a certain woman with a natural ability to command the stage, regardless of what she tells herself."

Sophie's stomach rolled, and she stared up at him in both horror and intrigue at what he was about to say. Part of her rejoiced. Part of her was terrified.

His eyes softened and turned to a warm, smoldering emerald. "Sophie, I know you tell yourself that this isn't what you want, that your life is safe while mine is too spontaneous and wild, but I know what I saw and what I experienced for the several days you were with us. I know you love this as much as I do. And aside from all that, having you around calms me, steadies me, gives me a bit of normalcy in my chaotic world. Perfect balance, remember?" He threaded his fingers through her hair and sighed. "If you crave this the same way I do, you have a place with us. I know it would be life-altering, but we want you to be a part of Shadows Rising, and if you're willing to take the leap, I promise I won't let you fall. Trust me, Sophie. Please."

She continued to stare because she didn't know what else to do. He may as well have been speaking Swahili. All of this was so outlandish.

"If you decide that you don't want this, it's all right. I'm not going anywhere, and we can figure something out. But if you decide to listen to yourself, to that voice deep inside of you, and if you decide that you *can* trust me to make sure everything is all right..." He spanned his arm behind him to indicate the stage. "We're waiting for you to take your place." He leaned down and pressed a soft, chaste kiss to his lips, then left her there while he went back over to the others.

Sophie stood there, not knowing what to do and feeling more lost than she ever had. He was offering her a once in a lifetime opportunity. To be a member of her favorite band, to see the world, to play music every night of her life! To be with him...

But her students... She couldn't leave them behind. Besides, what was she thinking? Was she out of her mind? She couldn't just go off and become a rock musician in a metal band. She had obligations. She had a life here. It was silly to even entertain that thought. She was not the rock star type. She was a teacher. She had gone to school to become a *teacher,* not a rock star.

She shook her head and tried to get a clue even while that meddlesome voice in her head was telling her that she was out of her mind for blowing this opportunity. *You want Zane, and you want some of the fun that life has to offer. It doesn't mean you're going to become a drug addict or an alcoholic. You can still be responsible, but be so doing something incredible that you never imagined you would get the chance to do! And you would be able to do it alongside the man you love!*

Love? Wait, *love*? She couldn't love Zane! Was she a complete lunatic? She barely knew the man!

She squashed that annoying voice, squared her shoulders and turned to her students. "Okay, guys, let's go find a place to sit for the show."

Elliott frowned. "You mean you're not going to join the band?"

She snorted. "Of course not. I have a life already. Let's go." She tried to shoo them away, but he was having none of it.

"Ms. G!" he exclaimed. "Are you mental? Anyone would kill to have this opportunity!"

She frowned, not liking that her seventeen-year-old student was trying to lecture her. "Yeah, well, I'm not anyone. Now, come on. You couldn't possibly understand where I'm coming from."

His eyes narrowed and he folded his arms across his chest. "Yeah? Why, 'cause I'm only a teenager?" He scowled. "Well, I'm smart enough to know that all you ever do is preach to us about how, if we have a dream, we need to make it happen. We have to go for it or else we'll regret it for the rest of our lives. We need determination and strength and blah blah blah. You go ahead and tell yourself that you already have a life and that's why you're giving up this amazing chance, but I know, and everyone else is going to know, what the real reason is."

She frowned at him in question.

"The real reason is that you're a total coward. You don't have the balls to do it because it's so foreign to you. Tell me something, Ms. G. How can you lecture us when you won't even walk the walk yourself?"

Sophie felt like Elliott had socked her in the gut. He may

as well have for the way all the air left her lungs. She felt nauseous for half a second as his words hit a place deep inside her heart she had been trying to run from. It was true. Everything he said was true. She hid behind her safe life because it was just that...safe. She had learned to rely on it. Zane and Shadows Rising was out of her comfort zone, foreign territory...dangerous.

She shot a glance toward the stage to where he was talking to Rhonda, and smirked as she remembered their bizarre and random meeting. Her cousin's chest and one antenna ball later, and he'd swept her off her feet and into his world of music and adventure.

She had only intended to have the one adventure, but who was stopping her from having more? Only herself.

A slow smile curved her lips as she thought of ending each night with laughter and conversation with him, of immersing herself in a world full of creation and art. Maybe it wasn't insane. Maybe it was like Zane had said...balance.

Suddenly, her doubt just stopped. It stopped fighting and stopped arguing, and she heard one thing from that inner voice loud and clear.

If you don't do this, you will regret it for the rest of your life. Take a chance, Sophie. Maybe you're not boring and plain. Maybe you're a rock star.

She glanced over at her students, who were watching the internal monologue play across her face. They got the message because they started to laugh and applaud. She giggled, shook her head, and strode over toward the stage. When she got there, she jumped up on it and went to Zane. She touched his arm, and he turned to her with a knowing smirk on his wonderful lips.

"So, Sophie," he said nonchalantly. "You ready to chase the storm?"

She smiled wickedly and grasped him behind the neck. "Ready when you are." She brought his lips down on hers and claimed them in a fiery kiss that set her whole world ablaze. When she pulled back, they stared into one another's eyes for a moment while the gym full of people shouted and cheered. She saw her future in those green eyes, and wasn't frightened by the possibilities.

Matt handed her a bass guitar, winked at her, and she

slipped the instrument over her shoulders. She sighed, feeling like she'd come home. She went over to her side of the stage, waited while everyone got situated, and caught Zane's eye when Billy did a four count on his drum sticks to indicate the start of the show.

He grinned at her, and her insides melted. She knew she had made the right choice. Every part of her welcomed and embraced this new part of her life. No longer plain, boring Sophie. Now, she was Sophie Storm.

She smiled to herself. *Let's do this thing.*

She played the first dynamic bass riff of the first song, and every piece of her world fell into place, then ignited like lightning and thunder.

About the Author

Brieanna Robertson

If someone were to ask me what I am, it could be summed up in one, simple word: Dreamer. Ever since I was a small child my imagination has run wild. I have been telling stories for as long as I can remember, creating grand worlds in my head and going on adventures that were invisible to others around me. Am I eccentric? Yes. Am I proud of that? Absolutely.

I write about the things that inspire me, both in this world and in realms only seen with the imagination. My heroines are sassy and strong. My heroes are sometimes shy. I have an obsession with music (and musicians) and a fascination with wings. I believe true love does exist, and sometimes it is found in the strangest, most unexpected places. I also believe that family and close friends are the glue that hold people together.

Above all things, I believe in being true to yourself and seizing the day. Life is an amazing gift. Make your experience as beautiful as you possibly can.